ACTING IN KINDNESS

ACTING IN KINDNESS

HAWTHORN ACADEMY BOOK TWO

D.R. PERRY

LMBPN

DISRUPTIVE IMAGINATION®

LMBPN Publishing
PMB 196, 2540 South Maryland Pkwy
Las Vegas, NV 89109

Version 1.00, June 2021
(Previously published as a part of the megabook *Hawthorn Academy: Year One*)
ebook ISBN: 978-1-64971-857-0
Print ISBN: 978-1-64971-858-7

CHAPTER ONE

"Hawkins, you're sitting this out."

"But, Coach!"

"Nurse Smith said there's no negotiation on this. You're sitting, end of story."

Coach Pickman stood in front of Hal, holding a magipsychic device out toward him. Her eyes and face were stern but a little ridiculous on her. She was five foot nothing, with a birdlike physique. Then again, physical appearance has nothing to do with magical power. For all anyone knew, she was the strongest magus on campus. That was Noah's theory, at least.

"Why are you giving me a chronogram?" Hal blinked at the device. Nin peered at it from over his shoulder, prompting the other familiars to have a look from their perches behind him on the bleachers.

"You're timing everyone today. And possibly tomorrow; I'm not sure yet." The coach tapped a sneakered foot, shaking the item she held. "Take it already, kid."

He finally did as she said. Hal might have been smaller and less advanced than the rest of us, but he was stubborn. That was an asset at Hawthorn Academy, from what I'd seen.

We'd need to be tough in this class. Noah had warned me about

Gym. Coach Pickman was a total taskmaster whose pep talks were angry at the corner of degrading—as if the boxy purple tees and yellow shorts we all had to wear weren't embarrassing enough.

"Stand up straight and pay attention, you maggots."

"I beg your pardon!" Faith glared daggers at the coach. Her nostrils flared. Something about being called maggot, in particular, set her off.

"There's no begging in this gym." The coach sneered. "I know your family well, Fairbanks. And if you don't want me to think you're a giant failure at this class just like Charity, you'll shut up, pay attention, and play your heart out."

"Woah, drama." Logan nudged me in the ribs.

"Pierce, shut your yap." She snorted. "I already know you're not a star like your sister."

I kept quiet. Noah had already warned me that I ought to keep my head down in here. Not that Coach Pickman ever made any sick burns about him. My brother got high marks in Gym just by following directions.

"If the peanut gallery is done, we'll finally get started. The name of the game we play here is Bishop's Row, and if you want to go anywhere with it this year, you'll do whatever I say and practice, understand?"

"Yes, Coach Pickman!" I didn't usually shout, but I was well aware that either this or "yes ma'am" was the correct response to one of her ersatz pep talks—or anything she said, for that matter.

"Morgenstern!"

"Yes, Coach Pickman!" I pressed my lips into a flat thin line to keep from laughing in her face as she approached. Remembering that if I wasn't so much taller than her this wouldn't be funny helped with that.

"If you can play half as well as you *comprendo*, you just might be the best student in this class. Everybody runs laps except Hawkins. You time them. When you've done three, report back here."

Running was something I was decent at, at least on flat surfaces like they had in the gym. There was nothing to trip over, no branches, statues, or passersby to tangle my arms or my feet. Just me, the track, and my long legs with their ground-eating strides.

It was tempting to bust out full speed at the beginning and impress everybody, but this gym was enormous—the size of a football field. Doing three laps at a flat sprint was beyond me and probably everyone else here, so I paced myself, which gave me a chance to watch the other runners.

Faith huffed and puffed, clearly annoyed at having to run laps. That was about what I imagined. But Bailey surprised me. She made the mistake I'd avoided, sprinting right out of the gate, but she was faster than I'd expected, possibly because she was an air magus.

I didn't know much about Alex Onassis, except that Professor Luciano had mentioned at attendance that he was a poison magus. He paced himself too, so either he had track experience, or this was all he had. He was tall, about my height, and wiry, so he had athletic potential but wasn't using it just then.

Logan might as well have been on the sloth running team. I couldn't even watch him because he was behind me. I wondered if worrying about his missing familiar was getting him down, or maybe he just had no motivation to excel at sports. Clearly, art was his thing, after all.

I lengthened my stride to picked up speed about a quarter of the way from the beginning of the second lap. I passed Faith with ease, slowly enough that I caught her eye roll. I just nodded and smiled, although I could have made a witty quip about having Faith that she'd finish before Logan if I weren't trying to save my breath.

About halfway through the second lap, I pulled ahead of Bailey. She winced as she ran, a clear sign she had overdone it already. I hadn't expected either twin to be a show-off. Until now, they'd struck me as almost extensions of each other, which was an unkind assessment. Clearly, Bailey cared about this extracurricular activity and being able to have her own thing, which made sense once I thought about it.

I was lucky Noah was a year older and had shared this information with me. The twins must have had trouble expressing their individuality, and I thought I had it rough, trying to figure out who I am. It didn't excuse either of them from backing Charity's cruelty, but at least I understood, kind of.

The only classmate left to beat was Alex. I measured my breathing, making sure I had enough oxygen to avoid cramps and the shakiness that plagued Bailey. After that, I gradually increased my speed.

There was something peaceful about running, even indoors. The feel of wind in my hair, hands and arms slicing through the air like a hot knife through butter, feet in a love-hate relationship with the ground.

It was just me and my body there, doing something simple. No mean girls or family secrets or dining hall disasters. I was in a zone, and it was the best I'd felt since getting here.

I stared down the track, the space ahead of Alex my ultimate goal. I was two-thirds of the way through the last lap, then three-fourths. That was when I knew I'd make it. I blew past my last classmate with feet to spare.

I was barely winded when Hal clicked the chronogram. Alex pulled up beside me, one sneaker dragging to squeak against the track. He leaned forward, placing his hands on his knees, then looked up at my face.

"Said you'd be the one to beat." He paused to take a few breaths. "Was right."

"It's all about pacing." I waved my hand vaguely in Bailey's direction. "She overdid it, but you're opposite. You never turned it up to eleven. The beginning isn't as important as the middle. Keep that in mind, and we'll be trading wins in the racing department."

"I'll remember that."

"Another thing is, we'll be a team most of the time." Hal scrawled some numbers next to names on a legal pad. "The laps are just to mark improvement. It's only this year, too. The next is another story. At least, that's what Dad said."

Before I could ask Hal what he meant by that, the coach came back.

"Hurry it up, Fairbanks!" Coach Pickman tapped her wrist even though she wasn't wearing a watch. "You're holding us all up."

Faith jogged slowly towards us, the last to finish her laps. Logan must've paced himself too, just at an overall slower speed. He came in almost neck and neck with Bailey, which meant he had stamina. Once we were all back, the coach motioned for us to sit on the bleachers next to Hal.

Coach Pickman picked up the legal pad and took the chronogram from him, eyes scanning the numbers before scratching her own notes under the list. She set them down next to a battered footlocker, which I immediately knew was full of equipment for Bishop's Row. I knew the rules too but decided that paying attention to the coach was overall less hazardous to my health than zoning out.

"Listen up because I'm only going to say this once." Coach Pickman glared in our general direction. "Bishop's Row isn't played with just any old sports equipment. It's not like your basketball, or your football, or your dodgeball, even though that one's the mundane version of the ancient Greek game this one came from. You gotta dodge the energy your opponent throws at you. Do this the right way as a team, you win. Do it wrong, you're out, and you screw your teammates over. Any questions?"

"Yeah." Faith said. She crossed her arms and looked sideways at Alex. "We have a poison magus here, which is unfair and unsafe. Does my father know about this?"

"That's why we've got this equipment." Coach Pickman slapped the top of the box. "It's protective and keeps the magic energy from hurting any of you cute little munchkins."

"Dude, rude." Logan looked at Faith like she came from Mars. "Nobody gets to pick their magic type."

"I'm used to it." Alex waved his hand. His eyes were half-lidded, a slight smirk on his lips. "Why aren't you?"

Faith's face turned an alarming shade of crimson. Her eyes narrowed, and her fists clenched. A gray haze emanated from them—undeath magic. Before I could stop her, Seth barked from across the gym, where he sat with the other familiars. She opened her hands, placing them flat against her legs. After a few deep breaths, she was back to her regular levels of surliness.

"Go and get those bands out of there. And call them ankyr from now on, except the one for your waist. That's the cestus. Directions for putting them on are in the trunk. After that, we get started." Coach Pickman turned her back on us, making more notes on the legal pad as she paced nearby.

Since I knew what to expect, I took the lead. Once the trunks were open, I started grouping the stretchy ankyr by size and setting them on the bench beside the trunk in heaps.

"Wow, you sure know this game." Logan pointed at the piles of ankyr. "I wouldn't be able to tell those apart. I mean, sure, I've seen them before since we host parties to watch the games at home, but that's it."

"It's pretty simple to play, just hard to master. The whole thing is an exercise in working together as a team, so we'll have to play to our strengths and cover each other's weaknesses if we want to win against the other class."

"I didn't think you'd be the jock." Faith snorted.

"Because she's a girl?" Hal raised his eyebrow. "How gauche." He made a gesture straight out of one of those teen movies, throwing in a selfie-style duckface.

"No, because she's a nerd." Faith rolled her eyes.

"What?" I blinked.

"Well, you got that perfect score in homeroom, didn't you?" Faith picked a set of ankyr up, pulling the smallest ones over her wrists.

"No, I didn't. Not from what I remember."

"See what I mean?" Faith shook her head. "She actually remembers the questions. She had to have gotten the perfect score. Definitely a nerd, and somehow a jock too."

"I'm serious. I didn't get ten out of ten. There's no way."

"Well, I didn't get it either." Bailey rolled her eyes. "Why don't you just admit it already—you're an evil nerd. Knowledge is power; everybody knows the bad guy is also smart. Every single time there's a story about a magus hurting people, the news always talks about their high grades or advanced degrees. Like her uncle."

"What a jerk thing to say." Logan gave Bailey a withering glare. "Well, I don't think you're evil, Aliyah. No way."

"If the idiot says it, it must be true." Bailey snorted.

"Whatever." Logan put on a good face, but clearly, she'd hurt him.

My temper and my temperature began rising, so I focused on getting everyone equipped. I'd be able to blow off steam when we practiced conjuring our orbs.

"So, Faith is right. The smallest ones go on your wrists. After that, the next size set of ankyr goes on your ankles. This medium-sized one is for your forehead, and the super-wide one with Velcro is that cestus the coach mentioned. You'll see it has a wide strap that leads to another band. Make sure you put it on with that on top and fasten the other part around your neck, like a choker. Oh, and one other thing—make sure the cestus covers your navel."

"What happens if it doesn't?" Hal asked.

"Projectile vomiting." I strapped mine on. "And that's the best-case scenario. Trust me, you want to avoid it."

"Noted."

Everybody got banded up. Hal even put a set on, practicing for next time. Once we were done, we stood in a line in front of the bench. Even with the goofy gym uniform on, I felt like a real athlete. Well, almost. The pros also wore wrist guards called ballistae to help with channeling and throwing accuracy, but that was a post-Reveal addition to the game.

"Good job banding up." The face the coach made gave me the impression she was almost unhappy we had done a decent job. "Hold your hands like this now."

She turned her right hand palm-up between her navel and her solar plexus, cupping it, then positioned her left hand on top with the same curve. It looked like she was holding an invisible basketball, which was the point.

"Now you're going to make your orbs. We'll go over how important speed and power are another day. For now, you just have to make the damn things, so conjure your magic into your hands and watch what happens."

I'd done it before, so I took the lead yet again. It looked like that would be par for the course in Gym so far, although I'd hoped it would be different. Keeping your head down is hard when nobody else steps up.

I felt heat before I saw the fire as I called on my magic. The energy from one hand pushed against the energy in the other, opposing forces that caved in on each other, making a ball. It's supposed to go clockwise, turning in the same direction as time.

Except mine didn't. Instead, it went in the opposite direction, and I knew from experience that was not normal for me.

"Are you a southpaw, Morgenstern?" Coach Pickman asked.

"No, ma'am." I shook my head but kept up the flow of energy in the backward ball it produced. After all, she hadn't told me to stop.

"Ambidextrous?" She followed up.

"I'm not sure." That was true. I never tried using my left hand instead of my right for writing, anyway.

"Well, your brother is a southpaw, and he's one of the best players in his year. Widdershins balls are easier to throw curves with but harder to control sometimes. Whatever works, you do it." The coach clapped her hands, pacing down the row of students. "Make it snappy, get those balls going."

"Oh! I feel something!" It was Alex. Sure enough, slick green energy whirled between his hands—clockwise, of course.

"Keep conjuring, kiddos." The smirk Coach Pickman made wasn't entirely unkind until her gaze fell on Bailey. "What's your holdup?"

"I got injured yesterday." She showed off her hand, the palm still covered with an extra-large Band-Aid.

"There's no note from Nurse Smith. Conjure already."

"I said, I can't." Bailey's lip trembled.

"Should I call him, then? Or maybe your mommy?"

Bailey shook her head. After that, she put her hands in the correct positions, and sure enough, almost right away, she held a whirlwind between her palms. It must have hurt since she grimaced the entire time.

"See? That wasn't so hard."

Logan made his water ball with no trouble. This was probably something he'd done on stage before because it was pretty and flashy. Faith's magic ball didn't appear even though her hands were in the right positions, her face placid.

"Good job, Fairbanks." Coach Pickman nodded. "You've outdone your sister on this one."

"Huh?" Hal blinked.

"Undeath magic is gray normally." The coach pointed slightly off to the side of Faith's hands. "It's off-kilter in an orb, and barely visible. You need to look left of center to see it. This magic is well suited to Bishop's Row. The opposite team will have trouble getting out of the way in time. Now all Fairbanks has to do is move faster than a turtle."

Her face reddened, eyes too shiny. I knew stifled tears of rage when I saw them, so I decided to use my jock privilege.

"I'll help her practice, Coach."

"Good."

"What?" Faith's eyes widened, the glimmer of impending tears vanishing in the wake of her feigned outrage. "You mean I have to spend time with this jock/nerd hybrid?"

"You'd better, or risk a failing grade in this Special." Coach Pickman held up the whistle she wore around her neck. "You'll learn to throw your orbs tomorrow. For now, class dismissed!" She let out a blast on her whistle, ending the session.

Logan and Alex good-naturedly punched each other's shoulders while I helped everyone put their ankyr sets and cestuses back in the footlocker. We all headed for the locker rooms, most in good spirits, except for Bailey. Even Hal looked excited in a tired sort of way.

"Totally unfair," Faith mumbled. But instead of rolling her eyes at me, she nodded.

Maybe our animosity was cooling.

CHAPTER TWO

I stood outside the cafeteria and took a deep breath. Going back in there after all the trouble I had at mealtimes felt like a bad idea, but I had no choice. This was part of our schedule. While I could opt not to eat, I couldn't skip it without the potential for trouble. I was already in this school's version of detention, so the last thing I needed was more disciplinary action and negative attention from the faculty.

I walked in alone and picked up a tray. Even though the panini sandwiches on order in the kitchen smelled heavenly, I avoided the prepared foods window. I didn't want to stand with my back to the door like an invitation, so I headed to the toaster and the bread.

I took out two slices of pumpernickel, then grabbed containers of sun butter and packets of jelly to make myself a sandwich at the table. I turned around to go back for the butter knife and napkins I'd forgotten and almost ran into Dylan and Grace.

"What's the rush?" Grace gestured at my tray. "Don't you want a hot lunch?"

"Maybe when it's pizza day." I shrugged. "Pizza is faster than panini."

"Well, you can always wait with us." Dylan gestured at the window where the food prepared on request come out. "But this lunch hour is only for our year. No upperclassmen allowed."

"Yeah, no need for sun butter and jelly sandwiches unless you actually like those." Grace wrinkled her nose.

"I'd rather have a panini." I nodded and went with them, keeping the food on my tray.

I couldn't put the bread back in the bag without it being gross for the next person and didn't want to throw it out, so I grabbed a brown paper bag from the stack by the breadbox. These ingredients would make a great snack later.

At the window, Grace ordered ham, Swiss, and mustard on rye. I ordered turkey and avocado on pumpernickel. It's my favorite bread. Dylan went totally overboard, ordering what I could only describe as a Frankensandwich.

"Hi there, Steve." He worked for the cafeteria, so of course, he knew this guy by name, or maybe he just cared about the other folks working here. "I want bacon, ham, chicken salad, turkey, roast beef, and one slice of every cheese you've got. Oh, and hot sauce too, if that's okay. Put it on a hoagie roll and bake it 'til the cheese melts. And don't go easy on that hot sauce, please."

Steve the sandwich professional started humming *You're Welcome* from *Moana*. You know, the song the demigod sings? Judging by the delicious scents wafting from the kitchen as he worked, he just might have had culinary magic. I'm kidding. No such thing exists.

"Are we secretly being recorded for that crazy reality show? What's it called again?" Grace snapped her fingers. "*The Biggest Eater*. Did I get that right?"

"You did, but nobody's filming. It's just that between work all morning, then class, plus having Gym before Creatives, I'm freaking starving. Like, my stomach's threatening vengeance on the Dylan Nation."

"Speaking of Gym, how did it go for you guys?" I only asked my friends a friendly question. I wasn't spying on their strategy and skills like Richard Hopewell might have. At least, I hoped I wasn't. Ugh.

"We don't have Coach Pickman, so we have it easier than you."

Grace feigned a shudder, then grinned. "Coach Chen is super chill. I heard he didn't even yell at Darren last year when he refused to run laps."

"Pickman's a taskmaster for sure. Judging by my class's experience, I think the twins might be the weakest link when we start playing." I told them about Bailey's overzealousness and then her reluctance to make her magic orb. "But I probably shouldn't be telling you all this since we'll compete against each other soon."

"It's almost like you're totally evil, fraternizing with the enemy and all." Faith elbowed her way between Grace and me, bellying up to the window. "BLT on wheat," she said to the worker behind the counter. She didn't say please or look them in the eye, and she called me evil?

"What's that supposed to mean?"

"Don't get all bent out of shape." Faith turned around, shaking her head. I'd have taken it as a gesture of superior defiance, but her shoulders drooped. "I've got resting- bitch everything and I hate breaking a sweat. Sarcasm's my only skill. It's not personal."

Somehow the BLT was done before the rest of our food order. Probably because of Dylan's famous Frankensandwich. In any case, Faith stalked off, taking a detour by the self-serve soup urns.

Our order came out so we all thanked Steve again and got our sandwiches, heading for the booth Hal already sat in, waving at us. He got up, so I took that as a sign that he wanted to sit on the outside. Eventually we're seated, Grace against the wall beside Hal and me next to Dylan on the outside.

All Hal had in front of him was a standard coffee mug filled with what looked like wonton soup. He lifted the cup wearily, almost as though it were too heavy, drinking down the last dregs of broth. After that he leaned back like he's exhausted from a hike through the desert and the soup in his cup was the first water he'd had in ages.

After that, the strangest thing in the world happened. Well strange for Hawthorn Academy anyway. Faith Fairbanks, self-styled resting bitch everything, marched up to our table. She looked Hal straight in the eye before setting an entire bowl of wonton soup down in front of him, along with chow Chow meinMein noodles and a big spoon.

"You need more than a lousy coffee mug if you're going to get better anytime soon. Eat your lunch and don't say I never did anything for you." She turned her back to us and flounced away, the flowing kneelength skirt she wore flipping with her legs as she walked.

Hal stared after her, almost mesmerized. Or maybe that's just how he looked every time he's a combination of surprised and under the weather. Someday I might know him well enough to say one way or the other but not yet. We all watched as Faith took a seat at the table with Alex, Lee, and lanky magus with glasses and curly hair who I didn't recognize. He must have been from the other class. Maybe he was Alex's roommate. Eventually I'd find out, I suppose.

Dylan tapped me on the shoulder and took a deep breath, about to speak. From my experience socializing with him this summer, I knew that look meant this was something important. But before he could say a word, we get interrupted.

"Hey guys, is there room for me?" Logan held a tray full of food.

Even though he obviously spoke to me directly, I didn't pick this table out. I looked to Hal for his decision.

"Yeah probably," he turned to Grace, "is it okay if we make room for Logan?"

Grace nodded, her mouth too full of food to speak. Just as they finished shuffling around enough to make space, the twins surrounded Logan. They were all smiles, the fake plastic kind.

"Oh no, Logan." Hailey said. "You've just got to come sit with us."

"But--"

"No really, there's someone who wants to meet you. Another fire magus." Bailey batted her eyes. "Please, she practically begged us to bring you over and introduce you."

"Go on." Hal nodded. "But there's always a place for you here if you need it."

Logan grinned back, then walked away with the twins. His shoulders remained high and tense. They headed for a table with the girl with the sphinx. She looked surprised to see Logan and I guessed the twins lied to get him over there. Of course, her cat wasn't with her. All our familiars were having their own lunches in the corner.

Something I failed to mention earlier about mealtimes was this. Our familiars got fed three times per day. In the morning, in our rooms. Their food appeared along with the wake-up bell. This was why they weren't hungry while we had breakfast. They got their third meal between class and our dinner hour. Folks stuck in Familiar Bonding fed their critters there.

Lunch was the only meal they needed to take while we ate. That's one reason the lunch periods were broken up so it was only served to one year at a time. Also, with customized hot lunches, it was easier on the cooking staff to serve fewer students each hour. I'd bet the hazing between upper and lowerclassmen might have been another reason.

Our familiars ate in a designated area of the cafeteria. Food appeared the same way as in our rooms every morning. Which is to say via mysterious teleportation. I couln't imagine Headmaster Hawkins was personally responsible for delivering every dish of magical critter food throughout the entire campus. He probably had a Magipsychic device on a timer or an assistant to help.

Or maybe not, judging by his apparent stress level. Maybe he wasn't prepared for this either. In any event, it was a good thing the upperclassmen weren't here with us. Because none of us had our familiars nearby to help defend against bullying.

As I sat, enjoying the simple pleasure of lunch with friends, I realized this was the most peaceful meal I'd had since coming here. I could have gotten used to it but shouldn't. Only one third of all my cafeteria experiences would be lunches.

Dylan didn't try talking to me again until after we cleared our trays and set our dishes at the window for the cleaning staff. When he did, he got right to the point without preamble or hesitation.

"Aliyah, I have to talk to you about Logan's familiar. The one he's painting."

"Okay."

"I've seen that dragonetdragonet before." He sighed.

"Where? At the Willows?" I figured since I met Ember there for the first time, maybe there was a dragonet-friendly hangout on the premises that would have attracted Logan's wayward little friend. "Was he okay?"

"This is going to sound really weird, and I want you to just listen. Don't say anything until I'm done, okay?"

I'd always had trouble managing my brain's internal/external features. Interjections just kind of happened when I was involved in a conversation, especially one that was weird. I was about to tell him I couldn't make any promises until I looked in his eyes.

Dylan Kahn, the nonchalant fun-loving king of tension breaking, was scared.

"I might put my hand over my mouth because you know what happens when I hear a crazy story."

"Yeah, I kind of figured, but I think you're the only person I can talk to about this who'd remotely understand, and I'm freaking out. So, will you hear me out?"

"Are you sure it's me you want? I bet Hal would listen."

"No. I mean, I'm sure he would. He's a great kid with a huge heart. But you know more about critters than anyone else here who isn't a professor."

"Well, Noah—"

"Stop putting yourself down, Aliyah. And listen, okay? We don't have a lot of time before the next Special starts."

"All right. And I promise to keep my mouth shut no matter what."

"Starting over. I've seen that dragonet before—the one Logan is sketching for a painting." Dylan took a deep breath and closed his eyes. "I've been dreaming about him since I was a kid."

I didn't say anything, because that was what he asked for. Promises matter, so I waited. Whatever came next must be difficult to say. Dylan lowered his voice enough so the clink and spray of the dishwasher shielded his words from prying ears.

"And I shouldn't have been because my parents had me tested practically the minute my magic started coming in. My level of aptitude is average. I'm not powerful enough to have a dragonet familiar, not like you."

I blinked. I knew dragonets were most frequently attracted to magi of above-average power level or higher, but I'd never been tested and wouldn't have classified myself as such. Dylan had just paid me a huge compliment, and I couldn't even say thank you because I'd promised not to talk until he was done.

"Logan's making that painting so you know what his dragonet looks like. I know he's missing, and I'm aware that he got your help."

Right then, I wanted so badly to ask how he knew. He only specified one piece that he got from Logan firsthand. Was Dylan spying on his classmates somehow, or was I paranoid?

"But what you don't know is that they never bonded. His parents picked the flashiest dragonet they could find and put a collar on the critter for appearances because that's all they care about. So, what you think of all this?" Dylan's eyes were wide and wild. "I can't figure any of it out, and it's driving me to distraction."

Fortunately, my brain spat out a course of action immediately. Unfortunately, I wasn't entirely sure I should help either of the boys. Even if they were both honest and had good intentions, the entire situation seemed too hinky. Was it a coincidence? And for good or ill?

While I tried to ask questions in my head now instead of later, my mouth shot first.

"I think we ought to prioritize finding this dragonet. And when we do, the three of us go in a room together and figure it all out. Logan says he doesn't want his parents knowing his familiar's lost. Spouting theories, questioning ourselves, and assuming will only make this worse." I took a deep breath before continuing, "I'm going home on Friday night after Familiar Bonding and talking to Bubbe. Izzy and Cadence said they wanted to see you this weekend. I think if I invite Logan along also, we might be able to settle this off-campus, away from—" I gestured at nothing. "Walls with ears."

"You know, that's a good idea. Dealing with this off-campus, I mean."

"Did it help? Talking about it?"

"Just saying it out loud was a big deal, but yes. Thank you, Aliyah. You have no idea much you helped just now."

"It's about time I did something right here." I smirked.

"You know, just because you make the right choice, it doesn't mean it turns out in your favor. You can be perfect and still fail. Intention is more important than outcome."

"Well, now it's my turn to thank you, Dylan. Thanks for being a friend. It means a lot, especially here."

The bell rang, cutting us off from any further discussion. Ember came flying across the cafeteria, fluttering to slow and make a soft landing on my shoulder. As Dylan and I went our separate ways to our next Specials, I knew at least one thing for sure.

My own problems might have been the most obvious, front and center for everyone to see, but everybody had their own struggles, visible or not.

It wasn't a comforting thought because distress is never like that. But knowing I was not alone had a value beyond expression.

There was safety in numbers.

CHAPTER THREE

I was in the library with the rest of my homeroom. It was enchanting, an open area in the middle with two levels. A set of wide stairs led from the lower level to the upper, which was bordered by wooden railings. The walls were darker here than in the rest of the academic wing, but not by much. They matched the inlay on the floors, a semi-spiral Greek Key pattern.

Somehow, the spacious area felt cozy, more so than our dormitory rooms. Even though the square footage was large, the stacks and the overhang from the upper level conspired to give it a warm and homey feel. There were no individual study cubbies, only tables, as though we were meant to work together instead of squirreling away on our own.

A long counter with wooden pushcarts behind it took up the far-right corner, positioned on the diagonal so the librarians could see most of the study area. One librarian, a person with ice-blue hair, sat in a wooden wheelchair reading a paperback, a hawk perched on the high back. Carved murals adorned the walls behind the librarian in the chair, depicting downtown Salem blanketed in snow. After a brief introduction and tour by the other librarian, a rail-thin man with silver hair and a kindly face, we were left to our own devices, allowed to study or work on whatever we liked.

I headed back to the circulation desk because I had a question. I kept my voice down, in part due to the sensitive topic of discussion, but also because it was a library. Libraries. Quiet. Duh.

"Yes, we do have books on that subject." Mr. Ashford nodded, smiling. His teeth were healthy but slightly crooked, which made his expression charming. "And you can use the student index to search."

He nodded at a large podium in the middle of the library, under the chandelier. It had the largest and thickest book I'd ever seen on it, bound in shimmering iridescent fabric colored like either dawn or dusk. The material either came straight out of the Under or was enchanted with every type of magical energy. As I watched, Faith approached it, bending at the waist, and addressed it.

"Bishop's Row tips and tricks." She enunciated clearly, and after a half a moment, the index's pages flipped on their own, glowing in prismatic color as the magic enchanting it activated.

"It seems the student index is already in use, so I will help you, Miss Morgenstern." Mr. Ashford pulled a smaller index out from under the counter, set it on the table, and began searching through it.

He did this with a level of respect and care that told me that books, even ones with long lists and nothing more, were extremely important to him. Mr. Ashford lifted his iridescent rainbow-framed glasses and pursed his lips, peering under them as he bent his head over the volume. His face was mostly unlined. From this angle, I realized his silver hair was an intentional choice and not due to aging.

"Here it is." Without looking up, Mr. Ashford reached out for a pencil and a blank index card. He jotted a series of numbers on its surface. "Scientific studies of dragonets and their ways, behavioral." He held the card toward me, straightening and smiling again.

"Thanks so much, Mr. Ashford." I smiled back. "I appreciate your help."

"May you find what you seek." His statement would have seemed ominously cryptic if it weren't for his friendly tone.

Because the tour was fresh in my mind, remembering where the section I was looking for was located was easy. Everything was done by numbers, familiar from my old school because the extrahuman community had adopted the Library of Congress system in the United States. I walked down the space between the stacks and found that there wasn't much in the way of research into dragonets. There were plenty of books on their anatomy and abilities, but little about their behavior and interactions with magi.

Being rare and special is awfully inconvenient sometimes.

There were only three books that fit my criteria. The bad news was, it limited the amount of information I could get. The good news was, I could carry all of them by myself in one trip. They were even on the middle shelf, which was a happy little accident.

I took my treasures to a table directly under one of the lower-hanging light fixtures, still wrought iron with solar globes but cozier. Two of those editions had been rebound and had old and yellowed pages. Without adequate lighting, they'd be difficult to read. I, of course, had my very own light source, portable and always literally at hand, but books were flammable, and I didn't want to risk damaging any of them.

Fire alarms were a thing here, too. Being suspected of arson was not something I wanted to go through again.

At first, I wasn't sure how to pull the chair away from the table. It was stuck to the floor. Well, that wasn't entirely accurate. The chair's legs were part of the floor, as though it was carved from or had grown out of the hardwood underfoot.

When I set my hand against its back, however, the chair came loose, or perhaps the floor released it. Either way, I could move the seat and use it, pulling it close enough to the table's edge to get some reading done.

I opened the first tome and began skimming the table of contents. It was a collection of academic papers, studies done on dragonet familiars and the magi who worked with them from various institutions of higher extrahuman learning. The titles of the papers were convoluted, which, according to Bubbe, was always the case when it came to this sort of publication, as though the wordier the title, the more likely it would be accepted into an academic journal.

This book contained twenty articles. After deciphering their titles, I realized only three had anything to do with dragonets as familiars. I flipped to the first, intending to mark it along with the others for later reading, but I got totally distracted. The author of this particular study was none other than Professor Luciano. No, wait—the given name was female, and the article was from the 1920s, so it had to be his mother or maybe an aunt.

I still marked it with a scrap of the index card but took a moment to read the abstract. I had a theory. Was this why my homeroom teacher had said he was excited to have me in his class?

Maybe he wanted to study me, and Ember too. What if he was trying to expand on this family member's research? Science was all about standing on the shoulders of giants, after all.

This idea might have disturbed some people, but I immediately began trying to figure out how to use it to my benefit. Maybe the mean girls were right, and I did have the makings of some sort of evil overlord.

I couldn't quit trying to get by here. People needed my help, and I'd promised it to some of them, so I couldn't abandon them just to salvage my failing reputation with faculty and the vocal minority of the students.

Did true kindness require total selflessness? After all, I was doing this research for two other people besides me. Bubbe always says you can't save a man from the ocean if you're drowning along with him. Until now, that had made little sense. I didn't mean any harm, so how could it go wrong?

But wasn't the road to hell paved with good intentions?

"Shut up." Oops.

"Shush!" It was Bailey. Because, of course, it was. "Logan's trying to study."

"No, you shush." Faith leaned a hip against my table. "Because she was already telling herself to be quiet. She doesn't need your help. If you don't like it, take the pretty boy over to the other side of the library already."

I sat there stunned, blinking up at Faith. She looked back down, first at my face, then past me to see what I was reading. I didn't know if it was nosiness or part of some information-gathering scheme. Maybe it was just a casual glance, totally normal.

But there was no question when she looked back at my face, meeting my gaze again. She'd seen what I was studying although she couldn't possibly know why, and I had no idea what she'd do with that information. She'd seen Logan's art project in Creatives. If she'd over-heard any of my conversations with Logan or Dylan, she'd suspect something was off. Logan could get into serious trouble with his family if she said anything. I wasn't having that, so I did the only thing I could.

I stood up to move myself and my research away from Bailey's and Logan's presence. Somehow, I managed this feat without closing the tome Faith had glanced at because nothing makes people think you want to hide something like slamming a book in their face.

As I walked past Faith, I leaned my head slightly in her direction and murmured my thanks. I wasn't snarking at her, I was grateful. Also, I figured it'd distract her from my readings on dragonets and why they bothered bonding with magi.

I'd apparently made the right call because she left me alone. I let Bailey and Logan stay where they were and schlepped to the other side of the library, to a table under the second level's floor. The library period was maddeningly short compared to Creatives and Gym. I had to get a move on.

On this side of the library, the light was dim. It was so low I couldn't read the old book without trouble, but the word "can't" hadn't stopped me so far. I toughed it out, leaning my nose so close to the page I might as well have asked it to start dating me exclusively.

I tried to take the information in, absorb it, but visions of Charity and the rest of the cruel and usual crew griefing me about book boyfriends danced in my head. I closed my eyes and leaned back in the chair, about to give up on deciphering it, but one more try couldn't hurt. After all, if it didn't work out, I'd just check it out and read it in my room.

But when I opened my eyes somehow, the page was lit. Not from within or anything creepy like that. As I said, the school couldn't be haunted because of its position between planes of existence. This was a no ghost zone, so I tried to figure out where the light was coming from. Before I managed the seemingly simple deduction, Mr. Ashford shook a little handbell on the counter. It jingled as charmingly as sleigh bells in the snow.

"If you'd like to check any materials out, you've only got a few minutes. Please make your way to the desk, and we will help you."

I brought my books up. As it turned out, Mr. Ashford didn't need assistance from the other librarian because I was the only one borrowing books. That totally reinforced my reputation as a nerd, and I wished I didn't care.

Because computers didn't work well here, the library used a system only accessible to magi. The librarian went through the motions, writing dates on cards and sticking them in the pockets on the books' back cover. The ink flowed, glowing with a gleaming white magic that originated in Mr. Ashford's hand. I was reminded of frost-laced windowpanes. So, he was an ice magus. Cool.

We exchanged pleasantries of farewell, and I headed out of the room with the rest of my class. Next was Lab, which seemed straight-forward enough. I doubted Professor Luciano would give us much more on the first day than a tour and a list of safety rules.

I couldn't have been more wrong.

CHAPTER FOUR

The lab was brightly lit, open, and spacious, but its ceiling was not quite as high as the library's. It made sense because Hawthorn Academy had unlimited space to work with. Even with the severe deficiency of windows, which made me feel stifled at times, it was never claustrophobic on campus.

I was the first one in the room, so I took a seat at the front. There were two rows, with five benches in each of them. I needed to sit in the front because I didn't want to miss anything. Lab wasn't easy, and the only way through was to follow all the directions exactly. Front and nearly center was the best place for that.

Unlike the classroom, the library, and the gym, this room had space just for familiars. An entire section to the side of my lab bench contained perches, tunnels, and climbing trees for our critters. The intention was to keep them out of the way during experiments.

Ember flew directly to a T-shaped structure. On landing, she bent her head down and rubbed her cheek against it. The perch was covered with carpet, like the kind of thing people with mundane cats had in their houses. Ember loved it. We didn't have any carpet at home in our apartment or in Bubbe's office downstairs either. It must have been a huge novelty.

The next familiar to check out the accommodations was Nin. She scuttled along the floor, her back sometimes humping as she hopped part of the way. I never would've guessed Pharaoh's Rats moved so much like ferrets, but you learn something new every day—which was the point of school, after all.

Hal slumped on the stool next to me, which fortunately had a back. He looked exhausted enough to need it. The seats were swankier than at my old school. Like the chairs in the library, they were fused to the floor until someone needed to sit in them. Hal either forgot or was tired enough for motor impairment to set in. He leaned back a bit too far.

"Whoa!" His stool came free, detaching itself from the floor.

I reached out, catching and righting it before it clattered down. Hal sighed, shaking his head. Then he concentrated, moving the errant furniture before getting back in his seat.

"Thanks, Aliyah."

"No problem."

Hal nodded, and I moved my own chair over. Clearly, he wanted to tell me something. One of the few things I seemed to do right at Hawthorn Academy was listen to people.

"What's up?" I lowered my voice in anticipation of whatever he had to say.

"I've got a problem."

"Oh?" I waited. Also wondered, since people in my year kept asking for help. I didn't know what I'd expected here, but it wasn't this.

"I don't think I have enough energy to get through this lab." As he finished speaking, Hal let out the rest of his breath. He didn't take another immediately. I'd seen this before at Bubbe's office with critters suffering a serious illness. He was in such a bad way I considered calling the nurse.

"How can I help?"

"I can't do any actual work in here." Hal glanced down at his notepad, where his folded letter from Nurse Smith was tucked under the back page. "Nurse Smith made me promise not to use any magic for the rest of the day. But you're a strong magus. Would you mind being my partner so I can stay and take notes? I'll help with setting up equipment mundanely, too."

"Professor Luciano can't have us doing experiments the first day!"

"Yes, he can. He's not as fair as you—"

"Welcome, class!" The professor stood at the front of the room behind the instructor's bench. He smiled, hands and arms out, palms up in a gesture to match his words.

I blinked, keeping my mouth shut for now. Not fair? How? He was pedantic, but he seemed decent enough.

The rest of the students shuffled in, choosing their spots and partners. Bailey practically pushed Faith out of the way when she tried sitting with Alex, leaving her to pair up with Logan instead. They sat behind Hal and me.

The lab portion of our education here at Hawthorn Academy was rumored to be its most intensive element. At least I didn't have to worry about being picked last or otherwise ostracized today. Even Faith looked like she'd keep her head down.

"Today, we'll do a quick rundown of the lab safety rules and then a brief but exciting exercise." Professor Luciano pulled a three-ring binder out from under his bench. "You'll find one of these in front of each of you. It contains the safety protocols and a summary of each experiment we will run during Lab for the entire semester."

I checked the table. Although it had been solid before, there was now a rectangular opening. The loose-leaf notebook inside was an old Trapper Keeper, the sort of thing students my age had carried back in the 1980s. Mine was emblazoned with an airbrushed unicorn.

Hal held his up, smirking. Its design depicted a round yellow figure with a pie-slice mouth, chasing a quartet of blue ghosts. Because we were in a magical school, the images moved, the unicorn tossing its head and the yellow man's mouth chomping. I couldn't help but giggle a little.

The professor glanced at his shoulder, where his familiar perched. He pointed at one of the wooden outcrops on the wall in the familiar-friendly space. The Strix swooped across the room, landing precisely where he'd indicated she should go.

"Please send your familiars to the designated area if you haven't already. That is always the first step upon entering the lab, and part of our safety rules. If our experiments include them, I will instruct you as to when they can be called over."

He opened his notebook, which was emblazoned with a neon-pink heart, flipping past a clear protective sheet and the title pages. After that, he turned his back, gesturing at the wall behind him, which was blank and white. A series of numbers with words beside them and a list appeared on the board.

"Take out your notebooks and turn to page eight, *Safety First.*"

A rustle of paper filled the room as everyone did as instructed. The list was simple and straightforward, even for a magical textbook. The first part was about checking labels for ingredients and instruments. The second pertained to personal protective equipment. In the third, the one our professor had already referenced, familiars were to keep to the designated area. Finally, there was a note about not running experiments while impaired. No wonder Hal wanted help.

"Flip to the first experiment and gather the materials listed, along with your protective equipment. The supply closets are on the walls in the back of the room." The professor clapped his hands. "Go!"

"I can't imagine he'll have us do much besides search for supplies to learn where they're kept." I held out my hand and helped Hal down from the tall stool, which couldn't be comfortable for him. The poor guy's feet dangled, even with the footrest.

"Thanks." He took my arm, using it for balance until he got both feet on the floor. "But no. He's having us run something. I overheard at the end of the mixer. Didn't Noah warn you?"

"No." I blinked. "He hasn't talked to me since the orientation assembly."

"Wow." Hal shook his head. "It's lonely being an only child, but stuff like that makes me kind of relieved I am."

"It's just such a big change." I reached out toward the handle built into the wall and pulled a cabinet door open. "Coming here and staying overnight, nowhere near all my old friends or the rest of my family. And Noah acting this way."

"At least you're not alone." Hal peered in at the items on the shelf.

"The only good side to that whole equation."

"Yeah, at least I'm with my dad. Some people have nobody here." He grabbed a length of tubing. "This is on the list." Sure enough, the label matched the one in our notebooks.

"What about this?" I held up a wrought iron stand. "The engraving is worn, but it looks like number four there."

"Oh, yeah, that's right. Would you mind?" He handed me the tubing, swapping it for the notebook. "I'm feeling a little out of it, so if you carry stuff, I'll identify it, okay?"

"That's fine."

"Hey, Aliyah?" Logan asked. "Are there more of those tubes in that cabinet?" He pointed at the still-open door behind me.

"Yeah." I stepped aside. "The iron stand's also in there, so grab one, too. Hey, where's your list?"

"Faith has it, but she's over there." Logan jerked his thumb over his shoulder. "Her pup's being weird."

I saw Faith standing by the familiar area. She cooed at Seth the Sha, squatting beside what looked like a carpet-covered doghouse. I heard him in there, whining inconsolably and refusing to come out.

"Why don't you come with us? You need the same stuff Hal and I do, after all."

"Okay, thanks."

We continued looking through the different cabinets and occasionally passing other students. Alex and Bailey managed to collect everything and headed back to their bench first. It was almost like they were racing me in a non-athletic way.

I recognized the true purpose of this first lab. It was in part to help us get acquainted with the room, supplies, and where all the safety equipment was, including stuff like the sink and the eyewash and the fire blanket, typical parts of mundane laboratory classrooms as well.

Hal explained the eyewash to Logan after I excused myself. Carrying the armload of supplies back to the bench was easy. Once finished, I headed over to where Faith was still trying to coax Seth out of the weird doghouse.

"It's okay, I won't let you get hurt. Come on out, now." Her voice was thin, quavery, and anxious.

"Do you need any help?"

"Not from you." Faith had her back turned so I couldn't see her face, but it sounded to me like she was on the verge of tears.

Whatever had happened on the way from the library to the lab had upset Faith. Since bonds are a two-way street, maybe it was the other way around. She needed help, and I couldn't give it to her, but there was another option. I marched to the front of the room.

Luciano glanced swiftly down at his notebook, but I noticed. He'd been staring at me before I headed over there. I had no idea why, but clearly, he wasn't looking at Faith or any of the critters.

"Professor, we have a very frightened familiar. Can you help?"

"But of course." His brows drew down. "No one should do this experiment in such a volatile familiar-induced state. And you are helping other students follow the safety rules by bringing this to my attention." The wide grin returned. "Kudos."

While his words were benign enough, something in Professor Luciano's tone bothered me. It had since the first time I'd met him. Why? So far, I only had the vaguest suspicion that he might be studying me. That in and of itself shouldn't have been too upsetting, however.

I wasn't the only one who found him intimidating, so being cautiously formal wasn't unreasonable. Inconvenient, though. Having to question his motives while he provided my education was less than ideal, and maybe worse than that.

Was assuming he had ulterior motives cruel? And why? Because he watched us like teachers are supposed to?

That was what the mean girls did to me—make assumptions based on rumor and first impressions. I hadn't thought high school was this complicated or difficult back on the mundane campus I'd shared with Cadence and Izzy. The difference was how needlessly complex magus society is.

We held on to procedures and traditions that had served us when we had to keep magic secret, but things were different now. They had been for decades, so I wasn't sure why magi took so much time to adjust. Even vampires adapted faster, and they were the most legally restricted.

At the bench, I went through the motions and put on my personal protective equipment. Hal copied me. From the bench behind us, Logan did the same. At least I knew they'd be safe during the planned experiment, although I still doubted we'd do one at that point.

Faith's issue with Seth might prevent the professor from sticking to his plan. Even with his help, she was unable to convince her familiar to come out or calm down. She started hugging herself like she was outside in below-freezing weather.

"There's one way to soothe him and let him stay put." The professor headed to the front of the room, Faith following him like a tail on a kite.

Professor Luciano pulled open a drawer under the board on the wall. Inside the contents rustled, releasing an herbal scent. I recognized it instantly since Bubbe used supplies like these. Maybe she even ordered them for the school.

I'm talking about sachets used in extraveterinary medicine. Different varieties helped magical creatures in pain, shock, or distress. He pulled a pair of them from the drawer, then closed it and headed back toward where Seth was hiding.

"I'm sorry about this, Professor." Faith apologizing to anyone wasn't something I would have imagined, but there it was. She must have loved her little Sha.

"At times, the lab environment makes familiars nervous, some more than others. Sha do have the best sense of smell, after all. Certain ingredients can stress them, so I always keep my supply of sachets well-stocked."

He leaned down, dropping the little bundles of fabric at the entrance to the small enclosure. A few moments later, I saw a slightly curved muzzle with a wet nose emerge from the darkness. Seth opened his mouth, revealing a blue tongue. Almost everyone else in the class gasped at this detail, but I'd expected it.

"It's okay, boy," Faith cajoled. "You can take them in there with you."

He responded, snatching both sachets with an alacrity even I couldn't have anticipated. Seth was extremely swift for a Sha. They were mostly known for stamina. The whining ceased, replaced by a series of doggy snores as Seth's nervousness succumbed to exhaustion.

"I wish *I* could take a nap." Hal leaned his cheek on his hand, eyelids droopy.

He yawned. It was contagious. I added a stretch to mine, leaning back so I didn't knock any of our equipment over or bump Hal's head.

Out of the corner of my eye, I saw a flash of gold. I turned my head to see Ember fluttering down from the highest perch to the roof of the doghouse. She stretched out along the top, draping her wings on either side of the peaked roof in a protective gesture. My thwarted desire to help must have transferred to her.

Back at the front of the class, Professor Luciano instructed us to turn to the next page and read the experiment's instructions. He went on to explain them, which was nice because they weren't clear. The only obvious part was that the antler had to break down at the end. The description included archaic symbols straight out of an old English apothecary manual.

Calling it a difficult read was a gross understatement.

"What's wrong?" Hal peered at the text, jotting something down on his notepaper.

"I can't make heads or tails of this."

"Don't worry, I'm translating."

"How?"

"My mom taught me." He continued scribbling, glancing between the lab's instructions and his notes frequently enough for me to understand he welcomed the distraction.

He'd barely mentioned his mother, but he'd hinted he was only with his dad here. Probably Hal missed her, but I let it drop because I figured he wasn't ready to talk about it. I stayed on the subject of the lab.

"Am I the only one here who doesn't know how to read these symbols?"

"Probably not." Hal tapped his eraser on the paper for a moment as he mulled over a shape I could only describe as a fish hugging a hamburger.

"It's all surf and turf to me." Faith snorted, pointing at the symbol.

"You took the words right out of my brain."

"That's enough out of you, flame-broil." She flipped a lock of hair over her shoulder. "I was talking to Hal."

"It's the symbol for lime." Hal gestured with his pencil at the glass beaker with the antler inside. "Which makes sense if we want to dissolve that. That's going to be tricky because we need magic to combine it, but it says here that we can't use fire."

"'Can't use fire' is probably the best phrase in the universe." Faith turned her back on me, stalking toward Logan.

"I wish you were nicer." Logan bent his head over the instructions. "We'd have more help if you were."

"I wish you were smarter." Faith rolled her eyes. "We wouldn't need help if you were."

"I bet you think that's a real zinger, but I hear that line all the time, so whatever." Logan reached for the jars of ingredients he'd gathered on our journey around the room.

That silenced Faith. She was either stumped for a response or wouldn't bring something worse than what Logan had already heard. I hoped it was the latter.

Watching him, I realized Logan just had a different learning style. He lined up all the ingredients, matching the symbols on their labels to the ones on the paper. It wouldn't matter if he couldn't read them because he'd still get the combination right this way. Good sense, that.

"Now that you've all gathered the materials and equipment and have read through the instructions at least once, put on your protective devices. We're ready to begin the simple introductory experiment." Professor Luciano rubbed his hands together like he had applied lotion or contemplated taking over the world. "As you can see, we are dissolving a section of antler in a basic solution catalyzed by magical energy. We have twenty minutes to give it a try. I can't wait to see what you come up with."

The instructions told us how to set up the stand, tubing, and containers. Hal did all that without magic. I appreciated having a lab partner who actually helped. While he worked, I checked the ingredients and set them in order of use like Logan had, except using Hal's translations. That helped me learn the unfamiliar symbols and copy the notes at the same time. In fact, I did it twice, so Logan could have one later.

When Hal finished, it was time to make the formula, which was my job. I handed the beaker and antler to my lab partner, and he placed it on the stand with the tubing pointed down over it. It was easy to measure each powder and even easier to mix them with the yew spoon, but the rest, not so much.

All the ingredients had to be activated with magical energy after that. That was what Professor Luciano meant by a magical energy catalyst. It'd be a delicate process because my element is fire, and we couldn't use any in this experiment. I couldn't conjure it, but there was another way.

I thought back to the first night my magic declared itself. When I was almost fourteen, it came in a nightmare, one where I somehow got stuck in the Under, right in front of the Sidhe Queen. She dragged me away to her dungeon, a place of intense heat and constant solar glare.

Of course, I woke up from that screaming. I'd set my quilt on fire in my sleep. Mom came in and shut it down. Later, I'd asked her how because she's not a null magus, the sort who can drain the energy from any enchantment.

She'd done it by reversing her energy, the same way she'd have banished her own fire. One of the most important things she'd ever taught me was that a magus could banish their own element even if it came from another source, but only if it was weaker than whatever they could conjure.

So, the way forward for me in this experiment was to make a cute little mundane fire and banish it. Luckily, I had a plan.

I took out a box of matches, the wood kind, from the Hawthorne Hotel. I pulled one out, struck it, then placed it on a glass dish. I attached the round-bottom flask to the other end of the tubing, steadying it in the upper part of the iron stand. Afterward, I gathered magic energy into the hand still around the flask's neck.

The glass chilled in my grasp as I focused on the mundane fire. The lit match continued to burn, but how? My magic should have snuffed it. I looked at my hand on the flask.

I almost knocked the entire stand over and ruined the experiment. My magic had never been this color before.

Gold is a solar magic color, like Dad or Bubbe or Noah had. That was what glowed around the hand holding the flask—pure gold.

My eyes widened as I noticed my lab partner, my friend, and my frenemy watching. Maybe the lit match had attracted their attention, or perhaps they wanted to see how I'd get around not using my element.

"Queen's Glory, she *is* an extramagus," Hal breathed. The faerie oath stunned me, coming just after I'd recalled that awful nightmare.

"No shit, Sherlock." Faith rolled her eyes. "Told you."

Inside the flask, my impossible solar magic had turned the other ingredients to liquid, which reacted with the lime. The glass heated, contents rising up to the neck on its way to the tubing.

I was frozen in place. Who wouldn't have been?

"Miss Morgenstern," Professor Luciano's eyes widened. He noticed too. "Remove your hand. Quickly!"

The fact that he stared at the flask and not me helped me move, finally. He was concerned about my immediate safety, not that I was just like Uncle Richard after all. I managed to save myself from a third-degree burn.

The result was fast, though not immediate. Smoke, foam, and heat appeared in the beaker as the solution dripped down. We'd done it correctly and watched it dissolve, so at least I didn't flub things and give us a failing grade.

A shattering sound followed by a flashpoint of heat behind me signaled that someone else hadn't been so lucky. I turned on my heel, seeing Logan through a veil of rising smoke. His eyes rolled wildly as he tried to step away from the fiery disaster on the bench between him and the rest of the classroom. His arms extended in a posture that meant he was about to instinctively shoot water to extinguish the flames.

It's a chemical fire so that won't work. He's doomed.

DANGER: FIRE: LOCATION: LAB B

If the announce system cut on, emergency response would be too slow. So would Alex, running toward the closet with the fire blanket. I knew that after racing him that morning. The fire spread, raging toward the boy who had set it loose, and his back was against the door to a cabinet containing more flammable ingredients. I was Logan's only hope.

But only if my magic was stronger than this conflagration.

CHAPTER FIVE

I said nothing, just held my palms out at the growing fire like a traffic cop ordering it to stop. The gesture didn't matter much; it was the thought that really counted. I imposed my will on the fire, not the flames at its edges, but at its heart. There was no point in trying to reduce the leading edge of something moving this fast. I needed focus to banish fire, and the situation worked against me.

Everything was too distracting, from the gasps and horrified cries of my classmates to footsteps pounding in from the hall, to smoke working its way toward my nose and mouth, threatening to choke me. And that wasn't all—the fire had grown from conflagration to inferno.

It was impossible. I couldn't possibly have been strong enough.

Ember landed on my shoulders, one hind foot on each side of my neck. She couldn't banish fire, but her wings wreathed the sides of my head like blinders on a spooked horse, damping all that noise, letting me be in the moment, letting me focus on the signal. That made all the difference.

I called for intervention from the heavens and answered immediately.

My magic crushed the chemical fire. It guttered and sputtered, then caved in on itself and died. From under a layer of soot, Logan's expression eased out of primal terror and into an exhausted sort of awe.

My victory was sudden, total, and completely unexpected since I didn't know my own strength. Turned out, it was more than enough—and more than I should have used.

I dropped my hands and sagged sideways. There was nothing to hold on to or break my fall. I was going down and couldn't even swing.

"Gotcha." Dylan stood over me. I blinked up at him.

"You're not in my class." He got me halfway standing, supporting me under one arm. Someone else came in from the other side.

Grace snorted. "It's a fire. Everyone's in your class now."

"It wasn't my fault." I let them usher me away from the scene of all that glory and shame.

"It really wasn't." Logan came out from behind the lab bench, grimy but seemingly unscathed. "I did it. Used too much. Blew up the lab."

"Accidents happen, my dude." Dylan shrugged the whole thing off.

"Where's Hal?"

I tried looking over my shoulder but sneezed and didn't quite manage. A glance around told me everybody had evacuated, but I still didn't see Hal's short, stocky physique anywhere in the throng as we passed through the door.

In the hall, I caught sight of Faith and tried to flag her down because no matter how much we sniped at each other, she clearly cared about Hal. But she turned her back, ignoring me. I couldn't blame her, either. She'd been vindicated, right about me all along.

Tell your friends before she does.

"I'm an extramagus."

"What was that?" Grace tapped her earlobe. "Hard to hear in this din."

I waited until they brought me to a bench between classroom doors. Once seated, they fussed over me, doing a hack job of taking my pulse and peering at my eyes. Grace and Dylan talked over each other, arguing about whether to send me to the infirmary, but I cut them off.

"I said, I'm an extramagus."

They stopped and stared, not even blinking. Must have been totally shocked.

"Okay," said Grace.

"Yeah," said Dylan.

"You don't believe me?"

"We do." She nodded. "But I can't say we're surprised. Sorry."

"So why are you still here?"

Before they answered, a series of hissed and emphatic syllables from our right interrupted. Professor DeBeer and Professor Luciano argued while a tall dun-complected man with straight black hair and brown eyes stood by. He wore the awful Gym uniform and a whistle like Coach Pickman. I guessed he was Coach Chen.

"—can't believe you'd have them run one on the first day like that, Lucy." Professor DeBeer's nostrils flared.

Professor Luciano smirked. "They're quite advanced, Miss Susan."

"Don't call me that." Her lip curled in a sneer.

"Don't call me Lucy and I won't." His lips pressed into a thin, pale line.

"What were you thinking?" Her hands went on her hips, the motion nearly jostling her lightning bird from her shoulder.

"More than you, as always. And they handled it." He cut the air between them with the side of his hand in a chopping motion. His Strix flapped to keep her balance.

"You sound like a novice instructor, not a triple doctorate." Her hands curled into fists.

"And you sound like a hidebound old coot, not a dissertation failure," he snarled.

Coach Chen's expression was like a still pond, at least until Nurse Smith showed up. His eyes narrowed, lips pulling slightly down.

"Where are they?" Nurse Smith turned his head, eyes scanning the hallway. "The students who got stuck in there?"

"Here, Nurse." Logan raised one hand like he was answering for attendance. He sat on a bench, leaning against the wall, but still looked dizzy. "And Aliyah too, but she only stayed because I was stupid. She saved my life."

His eyes looked starstruck. Maybe they were just glassy from the smoke exposure. At least, I hoped. Or perhaps the light Nurse Smith flashed in them. He came at me with the mundane penlight, and I tried not to blink as he did his test. Sometimes the regular tools worked best.

"The two of you need to go to the infirmary." Nurse Smith planted his feet, ready to defy our objections.

"But Nurse, I should go back and help clean—" Logan tried to get up but couldn't manage it.

"You'll do no such thing." Nurse Smith tucked his penlight away in a pocket, then clapped his hands three times.

Finally, his familiar revealed himself. A crab crawled from the opposite pocket, somehow able to cling to the fabric. It scuttled down to the floor, then held its claws in the air, clacking three times with both.

We watched the critter grow. It remained close to the ground instead of growing taller, increasing its circumference and thickness of body and shell. I wondered how until I realized what Nurse Smith's familiar was.

A Karkinos, the same type of crab that had pinched Hercules as he fought the Hydra in the ancient Greek legends. I'd seen one at Bubbe's before, but not close up. Certainly never watched one change size like that.

"Mr. Pierce, do you need help?" The nurse tapped his foot.

Logan shook his head. In a moment, he pressed a hand to it, groaning, with his other hand over his mouth.

"I'll take that as a yes, but before we start, are the two of you going to help Miss Morgenstern, or should I call for more assistance?"

"Absolutely." Dylan nodded, his expression gravely serious. I wondered what had gotten him so concerned. It couldn't be me since I didn't feel that bad. "I'm game."

"Oh, yeah." Grace beamed. "Happy to help."

We watched Nurse Smith assist Logan to transfer from the bench to the crab's back. After that, we made a most curious line, heading down the hall past practically the whole school. They'd all come out of the classrooms to stare as we went by.

From behind us came voices of professors corralling their students and herding them back into the classrooms. There was no more argument from Professor Luciano and Professor DeBeer's direction, but I didn't think for one second that their issues were resolved. It sounded like a long-standing feud between the two of them.

I shuffled along between my friends, realizing how lucky I was. They'd stuck by me, even though I could have put them in serious danger at any time. I hoped they understood the risks, but maybe they'd never even heard of them.

An extramagus could tap more than one elemental school, unlike regular magi. Those powers came at a cost, however, and it was threefold.

First, there was always a catch, some hitch, limit, or restriction on where, when, or how an extramagus could use their power. I had no idea what mine was. Usually it took trial and error to figure it out. That brought us to the second point.

Extramagi had a harder time shutting their power off. I'd banished that lab fire easily, but a water magus had created it. When it came to flames I conjured myself, it'd always been harder to shut them off. Maybe it was not about focus after all.

Finally, the third and worst catch, the reason most other extrahumans didn't trust extramagi—they didn't have absolute power, but what they got corrupted them, and nobody was sure why. There was a general consensus on how.

All magi draw their element from the Under, through the barrier this very school occupies. The Under is a magical realm of pure truth. When shifters cross over, they're stuck in animal form unless one of the Faerie monarchs makes a talisman for them.

The going theory was that access to more than one element from the Under damaged their brain chemistry. I should have said, "we," because I was one and had better accept it.

We knew quite a bit about how the Under harmed brains because changelings took on their full faerie physiology by joining a court. After that, they spent a year and a day in the Under. It wasn't a political choice, but a matter of survival. If a changeling didn't tithe, they'd go mad.

Many went on to marry and have children with magi. Some of these had both a magic and a faerie destiny. When that happened, they could lean on their magic and supernatural bonds like joining a werewolf's pack. That prevented the madness for a while, but any changeling who was also an extramagus carried double risk of insanity. That was what had happened to Richard Hopewell. My uncle had waited until he was in his forties to tithe.

Magi had a human psyche and a human brain. Magic stressed brain chemistry. The human mind wasn't made to handle an all-access pass to all its types long-term, so by calling multiple aspects of universal truth into and through their minds, extramagi eventually lose them. Nobody's come up with a therapy or medication to cure, counter, or even treat it.

In the future, I'd be a danger to myself and everyone around me. Guaranteed. I was destined to hurt people when all I'd wanted my whole life was to help. As my friends escorted me down the hall, I couldn't banish mental images of them recoiling in horror and pain at the distress I would cause them in some distant future.

I didn't realize I'd been crying until they sat me down in the infirmary, although not the room from the day before. This one had four beds. Once I was situated, Dylan and Grace helped Logan into the bed across from mine. Nurse Smith dismissed them, but they didn't leave right away. Everyone was defying the nurse this afternoon. No wonder his expression was so sour.

"I've got Familiar Bonding with you guys later." Dylan leaned in the doorway, blocking it. He refused to be brushed off. Good on him. Nobody should put Dylan Khan in a corner.

"Yes, and?"

"Will you be holding it? You know, considering the other two students are out of sorts?"

"That's a good point." The nurse nodded. "They should be up to it. Just come back when it's time. I'll run the course in this room."

"Smashing." Dylan dropped a wink. Grace giggled.

"Now get out of my way, or don't you want your friends to get treatment?"

"Thanks, Nurse Smith." Dylan turned his back and strutted out the door, Grace following closely.

Nurse Smith rolled his eyes, then clapped his hands three times. His familiar clacked those claws like an echo, shrinking again to scuttle back up into his pocket.

"Thanks, buddy." Logan waved at the pocket.

A series of clacks and chitters came from Nurse Smith's scrub top. I was almost annoyed at his complete lack of humor, but he surprised me with a chuckle as he headed out the door.

Maybe he was only stern because he cared.

"I can't believe I got to ride on the crab." Logan's grin was lopsided but genuine. It made him wince, though. He must have had one hell of a headache. "Cool story."

"Yeah, awfully nice of the decapod to give you a lift." I yawned, then wrinkled my nose. I was so tired it hurt pretty much everywhere.

"Aliyah, are you okay?" Logan stared at the sheet under his hands, picking at his thumb. "You didn't get burned, did you? I don't want you to get hurt. Ever."

I blinked, feeling for all the world like some day-blind owl. All this time, I had worried about hurting people in the future. Logan was upset because he actually did, and I totally ignored it.

"No, I didn't get burned, but I'm not okay." I grimaced. "Feels like that time I belly-flopped off the monkey bars in grade school."

"It wasn't all that magic you called to banish the fire, was it?" Logan's face got pale, all the color draining out of it. He must have been sick with worry.

"No. Let's just say I know how you feel, not wanting people to get hurt and screwing up anyway." I hung my head, partly exhausted but also ashamed. "I almost burned down the cafeteria, remember."

"But you did that on purpose." He slapped a hand over his mouth immediately.

"You understand, then. I'm a horrible person." The pit of my stomach went white-hot, roiling like a school of salamanders were playing water polo in there. I looked up, expecting to see him recoiling in fear.

Instead, Logan looked worn out, like he'd cast major magic and almost fainted. And he was crying. Not like ugly crying; nothing about Logan could ever be that. But a pair of cowboy tears made tracks through the soot on his face.

"You're not." He sniffled. "Because you did it to protect your friends. You're not horrible, I just always say and do the wrong thing. I screw up all the time. Can't do anything right, not even thank the girl who saved my life."

"Did you catch it back in the lab?" I raised my eyebrows, leaning back. I still couldn't say it out loud. "The truth about me?"

"Yeah, and I still say you're not horrible."

Logan wasn't the brightest bulb on the tree academically, but I knew he was canny enough. He also had a bigger heart than I'd expected beating in his showbiz-perfect chest. I could have dismissed his opinion. It would have been easy and probably right.

No. Nothing right was this easy, so in a convoluted sort of way, I had to believe him.

"Thanks, Logan." It was my turn to sniffle. "It means a lot."

Nurse Smith came back, followed by Zeke, who pushed a cart. The nurse handed Logan a small plastic cup with a foamy blue liquid inside and instructed him to drink. The vampire CNA tucked a box of tissues next to me, then poured me a glass of water and set it on the bedside table.

They switched places, repeating their tasks and gestures, except the cup Nurse Smith handed me contained a flat gray liquid. It smelled like nothing. Not like water, which has some vapor to it. This smelled like nothing at all. Like *nothingness*. Like you'd imagine the void of space might smell.

I hesitated.

"Drink that, please."

"What's in it?"

"It's a nullifying medicine."

"No way!" Logan sputtered, the water he'd just tried to drink flying back out. Zeke handed him a napkin.

"Relax, Mr. Pierce." Nurse Smith directed his next comment at me. "You overextended yourself. This will prevent you from casting any magic for the next hour because you need a rest. If you try conjuring or banishing in this state, you could become too ill to attend school at all, and you'll be stuck in my infirmary for a week at least. You can either take it like Hal did this morning, or you can have a sedative and sleep, but that carries a risk that you'll conjure as you slumber. Ultimately, however, your treatment is your choice."

"Okay." I drank the medicine, which was easier than I'd expected. It also tasted like nothing. "I've had worse than this."

"Yeah, that Augmentin they give for ear infections at mundane doctor offices is awful, so I'm told." Nurse Smith put on a weary grin. I realized he probably had one of the hardest jobs in here.

"Thanks." I couldn't muster more than that because the medicine had me feeling a little off.

The nurse left, Zeke following. The vampire CNA glanced back over his shoulder, giving me a small grin and a nod. As they closed the door, I yawned, suddenly tired enough to take a nap. I looked at Logan because I didn't want to leave him effectively alone in here with his thoughts, but he was already out.

I could safely close my eyes for a few minutes, so I did.

CHAPTER SIX

I woke to the sound of the door opening, revealing Dylan and Grace. They'd both had a chance to clean up, which wasn't the case for Logan or me, but when I looked at him, I saw that Zeke had come back while we slept. He must have washed Logan's face, and probably mine too. I didn't feel grime when I raised my hand to my cheek.

"Hey, I brought some falafel sliders from the café." Dylan set two wrapped packages on Logan's bedside table and two more on mine. He sat on one of the other beds, pulled the table closer, and dropped six more on its surface. Grace sneaked in, snatched one, then sat in the chair at my bedside to unwrap it.

"Aren't you going to eat?" Grace jerked her chin at my untouched sandwiches.

"Just a sec. I only just woke up."

"Not stopping me." Logan's voice was muffled by a mouthful of food. He'd gotten his appetite back. I hadn't, but when in the infirmary, do as the less infirm do.

I unwrapped one small sandwich and took a bite. It was surprisingly good. I hadn't expected the café's fare to be anything special, but this was something else.

"When did the food in that little café get so awesome?" I dabbed the corner of my mouth with a tissue. "Not that I'd know firsthand, but Noah always told me to avoid it."

"They hired a new chef to work there this year." Dylan took another bite, chewing thoughtfully before answering. "He used to work down in Providence. Graduated from Roger Williams University in Culinary Studies."

"Bet he's expensive." Grace shook her head. "But the sandwich is so good, I can't believe he's not worth it."

"I hear they got him on the cheap." Dylan leaned toward us. "He got turned by a vampire, invalidating his restaurant's license. You need a totally different kind to run kitchens as a vamp, you know, and he was out of money. Couldn't afford the fees, so he needed work, and nobody else would hire him."

"That sucks." The paper wrapper around Logan's slider crackled as he clenched his hand. "So unfair."

"Well, stateside vampires certainly get the short end of the stick." Dylan sighed. "Not that they don't have restrictions in the UK, but it's worse here."

"I'd say the worst." Grace leaned back in her chair, rolling her empty wrapper into a ball. "In Canada, we don't have those laws. Not the ones prohibiting them from drinking out of bottles or cups in public or banning them from owning restaurants. Those are totally ridiculous."

"They're not, really." Faith stood in the doorway.

"What are you doing here?" Grace stared daggers at the other girl.

"Just setting the record straight," she said. "And because I just felt like taking Familiar Bonding."

"So, you think vampires shouldn't have rights?" Grace stood up.

"I didn't say that." She sauntered into the room and sat on my other side, which surprised me, all things considered. "But aren't we too young and uneducated to make that judgment? That's why we're here, right?"

"But you're an undeath magus." Logan scratched his head. "I don't understand. If vampires lose rights, they might take some from you."

"There's no use complaining about any of it until we can vote."

Faith smirked, but her eyes looked hollow. She was like a parrot, repeating things she'd heard without examination or thought.

"Anyway. I don't think I'll be able to eat two sandwiches." I changed the subject. "Does anyone want my extra?"

Grace snagged it before anyone else spoke up. As she ate, Nurse Smith walked into the room, accompanied by Professor DeBeer. They stopped to stare at Grace.

"Miss Dubois, you may go." Nurse Smith waved a hand at the door. "You're not required to be here."

"Can I stay, though?" She tilted her head. "All my friends are here. Well, except for Hal. Where is he, anyway?"

Professor DeBeer and Nurse Smith glanced at each other. I got the impression they didn't want to say, but we got an answer anyway.

"His father's taking care of him." The professor waved a hand dismissively. "At any rate, we need to get started if you want to be out of here at a decent hour to do your regular homework."

Nurse Smith clapped his hands, and his familiar strutted in with an enormous box on his back. From the noises, I correctly guessed that a variety of magical critters were inside. When the nurse opened the box, they emerged one by one.

Ember "peeped" from the headboard behind me and fluttered to the floor to join them, clearly excited. Lune hopped out from under Grace's chair, nose twitching as he raised his ears. I heard Seth stirring inside Faith's tote bag. She lifted him out and set him down. The Sha trotted over but sat a safe distance from the newcomers. Maybe she was here for his benefit.

A five-toed cat padded softly toward Logan's bed, bunching her haunches before leaping up to meet him. She sat at his knee, head craning forward as she sniffed in the general direction of his last bit of food.

A curly-haired poodle dog trotted toward Dylan, sitting at his feet and looking up. He cocked his head, lifted one ear, then shook it. He turned his back, although his tail wagged. Clearly, he wasn't impressed with the air magus. Poodles tended to favor earth.

"Come on out now, there's a love." Professor DeBeer spoke, coaxing the creature still in the box, but it stayed put.

"It's all right, Sue. Let's just get started." Nurse Smith carefully moved the box to the floor, then clapped three times. His crab did the clacking thing, then disappeared into the pocket.

The lecture Professor DeBeer gave was extremely basic. I'd heard it all before because she practically recited one of Bubbe's pamphlets on caring for a familiar and how it differed from a mundane pet. It would have been totally boring if Ember wasn't busy making friends. She already knew and liked Lune, but got along just fine with the poodle and the polydactyl cat. She even played with Seth.

I noticed that the Sha followed her, but the moment she turned his way, he pretended not to care. His behavior reminded me an awful lot of Faith's.

Professor DeBeer finished her portion of the lesson. Nurse Smith took over, asking us to give our familiars some basic commands. Dylan and Logan did this with the poodle and the cat. As they worked, the creature in the box finally decided to make its appearance.

The first thing we saw was a long snout and a bulbous pink nose, which I immediately recognized. Its wrinkly pink ears and gray fur were unmistakable, and before her shoulders emerged, everyone knew the little gray lady was a possum.

"Gross." Faith shook her head and rolled her eyes. "There's no way that is a magical creature."

"She definitely is," Grace corrected.

"You're correct, Grace." Nurse Smith nodded. "She knows precisely when discretion is the better part of valor, and is an excellent companion for anyone who hides their true self frequently. I hear they're a favorite amongst magi in intelligence fields."

"Interesting." Faith snorted. "Not. Still think it's gross."

The possum definitely wasn't ordinary. She had a red tail that glowed faintly. I wasn't a magical creature encyclopedia so her species name eluded me, but Grace was right. In moments, she headed straight for Logan, ears perked up and eyes bright.

"Oh." He turned away from the incoming creature, paying extra attention to the cat. "Um. You're looking for someone else, girl."

"Moving along."

I hadn't noticed Nurse Smith's note-taking during the earlier part of the lesson. The scratch of his pen against paper continued the entire time we practiced. He finished without having us demonstrate individually, which was a relief. Ember was usually well-behaved, but I couldn't handle any more attention.

After dismissal, Faith left. Logan and I were stuck until the nurse cleared us. Dylan and Grace didn't have to stick around but did anyway. After another check that took slightly longer than the one he'd given in the hall, we were allowed to head out for dinner.

I didn't want to go.

Don't get me wrong. I definitely wanted out of the infirmary. In fact, I was the first one through the door. But once we were in the lobby, I stopped, balking at the prospect of entering the cafeteria. I couldn't help it; I was afraid.

"What's up, Aliyah?" Logan stepped in front where I could see him before placing a hand on my shoulder.

"Isn't there any other way to get dinner?" I sighed. "Without going in there."

"I get it." Grace nodded. "Those sliders tasted amazing, Dyl, but they were tiny."

"Hmm." Dylan chewed the corner of his bottom lip, thinking. "You know what? I'm not sure."

"Are you guys talking about a to-go bag?" Lee stood at the bottom of the stairs, holding a paper shopping bag—the kind with handles. "Because I know how to get those. This one's for Hal."

"Oh, so you've seen him?" In the battle between hunger and concern, concern won. I'd better appreciate this trait of mine before it got swallowed by extramagus awfulness.

"Not yet, but the headmaster told me he's up in our room and can't make it down." He raised the bag, showing it off. "This is usually for second and third years cramming during exams, but they'll let anybody have one for dinner as long as you know where to ask."

"Wow, that's awesome." Logan grinned. "We sort of missed some stuff and have to study." He shrugged, lying easily about our reasons. That wasn't why we wanted to avoid the caff. "Where do we go for that?"

Lee gave us unexpected but somehow easy instructions. The four of us followed them, heading around the corner along the side of the staircase and then under it. We found ourselves in a tall yet narrow hallway. At least it wasn't a closet under the stairs. This hall was like something out of a dream, the confusing and only mildly disturbing kind.

The only door was at the end, which looked much farther away than it was. One little touch that had me instantly homesick was that it was a half door like the ones in Bubbe's office. My eyes stung, not from the smoke but threatening tears. I didn't want to cry anymore so I knocked, hoping whoever answered would shatter the impression of home and banish this feeling.

It worked. The door opened, revealing a matronly woman with a befloured floral apron. Her gray hair was tied into a low bun, over which she wore a hairnet.

"Hello, and welcome to Lunch Lady Land." She chuckled. "I'm Penelope, how can I help you?"

"Hi there, Penelope." Logan amped up his already high-watt smile. "We'd like some to-go bags, please. One kosher and the rest regular."

"Burning the mid-evening oil, huh?" She clapped four times. "Your food's on its way."

The woman pressed a switch embedded in the door frame. I knew from Bubbe's office that she'd activated an audio system. I shouldn't have been surprised that parts of Hawthorn Academy reminded me of the house I grew up in. They had been designed by the same magus, after all.

Unlike Bubbe's, the switch here didn't play music to soothe magic beasts. Instead, it was a lively polka with plenty of oom-pah. In moments, we heard hooves clopping on the floor behind Penelope the self-styled lunch lady, in perfect time with the polka beat.

A goat with curiously scaled horns appeared. He shook his head, then turned sideways. He was saddled with a set of panniers, which contained our to-go bags. One of them was marked with a K.

How'd they come out so fast?"

"Sandy's a Pricus." Penelope smiled, eyes gleaming with totally justified pride. Her familiar was extremely rare and very special.

"Oooh, a sea-goat!" I clapped my hands. "Cadence would just about die if she were here."

"What's a Pricus, if you don't mind my asking?" Logan treated Penelope like royalty, which for all I knew, she was. The headmaster's unorthodox hiring practices had taught me to stop assuming anything about his staff, including the ones in the background.

"They're amphibious creatures who have command of time for short spans, enough to get your meals out to you a full minute before they've been cooked." She beamed. "Thanks for asking. You might be surprised to hear this, but nobody's ever bothered in the seven years Sandy and I have worked here."

Penelope handed us our bags, and we thanked her. I took perhaps an unusual amount of time and effort on that since as far as I was concerned, Sandy and his magus were lifesavers. I could avoid Charity during two-thirds of my mealtimes now.

The rest of the week, meals would be on easy mode.

CHAPTER SEVEN

For once, I was right that first night at Penelope's window. The following days went far more smoothly than the disastrous first two. At breakfast each morning, Faith and Logan rounded out our table, making our numbers high enough that Charity couldn't do more than stare, point, and whisper cruel nothings about us in her circle's ears.

Said circle included Noah, which stabbed like a knife in the back, but I said things went smoother, not perfectly. Our summertime high hopes had gone down in flames, and there would be no recovering them now. Life at Hawthorn Academy for the rest of the first week was like applying cream to a burn as far as my brother went.

The other issue was all the bickering between our professors. Luciano and DeBeer hated each other for reasons still unknown, a fact they tried keeping on the down-low. By the end of the week, I didn't know whether it was a professional or a personal rivalry, but it was like one of those magic eye pictures, unable to be unseen and distracting once known.

Their issues made it harder on the six of us because our class assignments weren't the same. Instead, each scrap of homework or required reading felt like a series of escalations in an epic academic arms race. We couldn't even be effective study buddies. What was worse, neither educator noticed it impacting us.

By the way, you heard me right. I said there were six of us. Faith and Logan officially joined Hal Hawkins' little out-group. Logan still followed me around like he owed me his life, which I periodically reminded him wasn't true. But did he listen? No.

I looked forward to the end of the week when I could find his lost dragonet already, because our dynamic was already pretty awkward, and this new element only made it worse. It also pissed Noah and Elanor off, judging by the dirty looks we got whenever they saw us together. And the first day they'd practically tried to arrange our marriage.

Faith was just there for Hal. Whether she'd glommed onto him because he was the headmaster's son and she was making an indirect power-play or there was some other reason, I didn't know. Either way, she lavished small and random acts of ingratiation on him multiple times per day. Little snacks were common, but on Thursday she gave him a friendship bracelet, the kind woven from embroidery floss.

She only tolerated the rest of us, reminding me of the cat Izzy's grandmother kept. Mittens loved Abuelita but had a withering stare for every other member of the household. The only other person she showed interest in was Bubbe, who had literally saved her tail the time she got frostbite.

Like Mittens with my grandma, Faith showed a grudging respect toward Logan, which was surprising because when it came to anything academic, his unorthodox learning style frustrated her no end. My best guess was she felt a sort of kinship with him. His sister Elanor was almost as bad as Charity when it came to mean behavior.

Grace and Faith still came to Familiar Studies with us, even though they didn't have to. Faith wanted Seth to have an easier time on campus, but for Grace, it was a different story. She and Lune had the kind of bond Dad used to tell us about in bedtime stories—like a fairytale. While Faith stuck around out of necessity, Grace was there because she cared. Maybe too much.

Grace had a crush on Dylan. I couldn't blame her. He was kind, funny, smart, and one handsome dude. He'd turned the heads of practically all the straight girls in school, including Grace. She was also a super-supportive roommate, giving me privacy when I needed it. Without that consideration, I wouldn't have been able to have my rule-breaking calls with Izzy and Cadence every night.

Grace was awesome. I didn't think I'd have made it past day one without her, so of course, I supported her crush on Dylan whenever possible even if I did feel a bit regretful about not letting Cadence push us into a date over the summer.

Lee hung around with us too sometimes, usually for dinner and homework in the lounge after Familiar Studies. He was quietly friendly and his Sumxu was playful. When Scratch was around, all the animals had a blast, even the nervous Sha. Sometimes it was distracting, but their antics outdid the best cute animal vids available on the mundane Internet, so we never minded.

Speaking of our familiars, the strangest thing happened. Ember flat-out befriended Seth. Somehow, the two of them put aside the instinctive animosity between their species to spend the entire Lab period and most of Gym curled up together, whuffing and peeping at each other softly. Nin often joined them, but she seemed fonder of Lune. These other unlikely friends had what I can only describe as dance-offs. If you've ever seen a rabbit dance and a ferret hop, you have some idea of what that looked like.

If Charity's group was our enemy, Alex's was like Switzerland. He hung around with his roommate Eston, and Lee bounced between them and us. The twins almost always added themselves in that group, largely because they idolized Kitty, who appeared to be dating Eston. Why a fire magus would want to date a water one was beyond me, mostly because when I tried wrapping my brain around that dynamic, my awkwardness with Logan got in the way.

Technically I was an extramagus, not straight-up fire, but the two elements were opposite, and my second magic wasn't much better. Solar plus water had no reaction or synergy. Then again, my long friendship with Cadence the mermaid seemed to fly in the face of that.

Alex didn't give us any trouble and kept the twins off our backs, which was nice because they still hung on every word Charity tossed in their general direction. He never came to our rescue either. Lee spent time with us because he was Hal's roommate. Probably, he acted on his own. I leaned on the side of assuming he fell outside the complex ecosystem of Hawthorn Academy's cliques.

That said, having both the first years' small groups go largely unmolested felt miraculous. Charity's circle included the entire third-year class and most of the second-years as well. Among those who didn't associate with her were Noah's ex-boyfriend Darren. He avoided everyone in our year, too.

He had his nose in a book almost all the time, like the three other second-years who hung around him. They worked hard on advanced placement courses. Darren and company were often in a corner of the library when we went in for our period. The Ashfords never kicked them out. Otherwise, they kept to the lounge. We always saw them there, eating out of Penelope's to-go bags just like us.

Logan, Dylan, Hal, and Grace accepted my invitations to visit and either meet or catch up with Cadence and Izzy that weekend. The days crawled, nights feeling truncated like sleep took no time at all. I didn't dream at Hawthorn Academy. Neither did any of my friends who talked about that sort of thing. And mine used to be so vivid. By Friday morning, I found myself wondering whether I'd have any during my weekend at home.

The morning went by uneventfully with one notable exception. At Gym, Hal was finally allowed to join Bishop's Row practice. He made mediocre projectiles but was excellent at dodging. I suspected he was using his space magic for something other than conjuring his orb. If so, it worked for him. He'd be the sleeper star player on our team if he could only increase his stamina, but his skills would be perfect for last-minute plays and scores against the timer.

At Familiar Studies, Nurse Smith brought out the possum again. She tried befriending Logan once more but eventually gave up. After spending four days with him, I understood why. He was under enormous pressure from his parents to have a familiar who'd look good on stage and in promotional photos.

I wondered what he'd do if my hunch was correct and the dragonet Logan's parents had picked out for him bonded with someone else. As awkward as the life-debt misunderstanding between us was, I'd do my best to help him.

Instead of going to Penelope's door for to-go bags with my friends, I bid them goodbye. What felt like the longest week of my life was over, and I got my reward—a weekend at home, surrounded by my family and oldest friends.

I hefted the knapsack with my library books, some laundry, and in the bottom, the forbidden communication orb. Walking across the lobby, I almost expected some incident, either an ambush by Charity and company or walking in on yet another argument between Luciano and DeBeer, but it was quiet and mostly deserted. In the hall leading to the school's exit, Headmaster Hawkins paced.

"Headmaster, thanks for an interesting week," I said.

"Oh?" Apparently, I startled him. His eyes were wide and his hands clasped under his chin. "And you came all the way over here to say that?"

"No." I grinned, hoping to put him at ease, but he didn't relax. If anything, he looked more anxious than before. "Just heading home for the weekend is all."

"I see." This revelation did what my smile couldn't. He dropped his hands, still folded but at his waist instead, and the wildness went out of his eyes. "Well, have a peaceful time, then. Remember, the doors are locked early on Monday morning, so it's best if you return Sunday night."

"Thanks, Headmaster."

Good thing he reminded me since I'd definitely have forgotten that detail. I waved before pushing through the door and out into the sunset light on Essex Street. It took a moment before I got my bearings. The door to Hawthorn Academy had migrated again, this time to the blank wall across the street from a touristy t-shirt shop.

It was almost two long blocks away from Hawthorne Street and my house.

But this was my town and my street, one I'd walked countless times through most of my life. The cobblestones beneath my feet welcomed me, the uneven surface lifting my spirits until the spring in my step was practically ineffable.

Ember let out a series of musical peeps, and I shared her good cheer. She was less elated and relieved than I was, but she was content, and that was what mattered. In two minutes, I walked up the driveway behind Izzy's house.

Just like that, I was home.

CHAPTER EIGHT

I didn't need to knock or ring the bell; I had my keys. The hallway was dark, usual for a Friday night. Upstairs, I kicked off my shoes on the landing, then entered the living room. Ignoring the tufted sofa with its fleecy throws and cushioned comfort was easier than I thought. I was here on a mission, after all, but the house was empty. Mom and Dad must've gone out.

Sure enough, there was a note on the kitchen counter.

Gone to dine at Bay Bridge. Pizza on counter. See you later! Love, Mom and Dad.

Of course. It was live music night, so they were on a date. I'd never let them know I planned to spend the weekend here or asked the school to do so on my behalf. They had no idea whether I'd come home, although last year they'd figured Noah wouldn't after the first week. My parents demonstrated their love by leaving food out anyway.

Last year, I was home alone while they went on their Friday night dates, but they always left more for dinner than I could eat, probably in case Noah felt the need to escape campus for even just one meal. Of course, they understood. Both of them had attended and graduated from the same school, after all.

I leaned against the counter, not bothering to sit at one of the stools, and ate lukewarm pizza over one of the plates they'd left with the box. Ember perched nearby, devouring the slice I'd set aside for her.

It was from Engine House, reminding me of slices grabbed all summer. I'd be sure to take my school friends there during the weekend, which meant plenty of pizza for everyone.

Once my stomach was no longer growling, I decided it was time to visit Bubbe. The light was on in her office, so she was there, but first, I needed to put the contents of my knapsack away. It wouldn't do for either of my parents to find the seaglass, and I wanted to do some laundry. I left Ember on the counter to finish her dinner.

I headed upstairs to my room, stowing the orb in my closet behind a bag of winter clothes. Once that was done, I set the library books on my bedside table. As I stood, I bumped my head, of course. I'd almost forgotten that low ceiling, which wasn't a problem at Hawthorn.

All the same, that was my room, my home. I belonged here, gabled roof and all. But it was time to leave it for the moment, at least. I carried the knapsack into the upstairs bathroom, opened the laundry hatch, and dumped the dirty clothes down the chute. After closing it, I returned the pack to my room and headed back downstairs.

The laundry machine was in the downstairs water closet, a stacked unit with the washer on the bottom and the dryer on top. I took my clothes out of the hamper under the chute and tossed them in the washer, then dumped some detergent in on top. I was supposed to do it the other way around. My generation wasn't killing household chores. I was just in a hurry, wanting to catch Bubbe before she turned in for the night.

I started the washer, knowing this cycle would give me an hour before I needed to put the clothes in the dryer. That would be enough time to chat with my grandmother downstairs.

"Come on, girl." I beckoned to Ember. She leaned against the paper towel holder, stomach distended, with an enormous grin on her scaly little face.

"Peep?" Of course, she wondered why we were leaving when we just got there.

"Were going to go see Bubbe. You'd like to see Bubbe too, right, girl?"

She stood up, fluttering her wings with excitement, but they didn't manage to lift her off the granite surface. After a few frustrated peeps, she made her way toward the edge of the counter and sat looking up at me expectantly.

"Okay, I get it. Pizza belly means you need a little help." I chuckled, stretching my hands out to lift her up to my shoulder, where she draped herself around the back of my neck.

I felt her rounded tummy against my left shoulder where I usually carried my knapsack. Ember weighed way less, even though she'd totally pigged out.

I headed down the back stairs and knocked on the service door for Bubbe's office. I heard voices inside, more than just my grandmother's. Maybe she had an emergency visit or a friend over. I waited patiently and listened to her footsteps coming down the hall toward the door.

"Aliyah, this is a surprise." Bubbe smiled.

"I'm sorry, Bubbe. I'll come back later if I'm interrupting anything."

"No, you're not. I do have some friends over, but you've met one of them before, and I've just been saying how I'd like to introduce you to the other." She pulled the door open wider and stepped aside to let me through.

We walked down the hall toward the kitchenette and break room, the place where she sat with clients to discuss issues with familiars beyond those of a physical nature—and where she brought them when there was nothing more she could do to help.

That was one reason it was fully equipped with a range, oven, sink, and refrigerator. The table had four chairs and enough room for the yellow and white earthenware tea set, which was in use that evening. Bubbe always said kitchens were the one room where anyone felt like they could sit down and talk.

Which was abundantly true that night. "Anyone" was a great way to define the diversity of Bubbe's guests. She'd mentioned before that I'd already met one, but only in a very vague way. Because, although I instantly recognized Dr. Elizabeth Rassmussen from photographs, I couldn't possibly remember her from the one time we met. I was still in diapers back then.

Of course, she looked exactly the same despite the passage of so many years. Round-faced, straight honey-brown hair, eyes that twinkled like the moon on frost. Dr. Liz was a vampire, the one I mentioned earlier from New Hampshire. Bubbe had pictures of her in her office, mostly ones with them at professional conferences. They were colleagues and friends.

I'd never seen the rotund older gentleman seated at the kitchen table before, but I instantly recognized the creature with him.

"Oh! It's the Grim." I couldn't help but smile and wave. "Hello again."

The shadowy canine thumped its tail on the floor, rapidly sitting up and cocking their head. Grims are pure faerie creatures, which meant this one was genderless and responded to they-them pronouns. It'd be rude to call them "it." But anyway, the man was no magus. Grims couldn't be familiars, but they did make contracts with psychic summoners.

"Dr. Brodsky, this is my granddaughter Aliyah."

"I've heard so much about you. It's lovely to finally make your acquaintance." His voice was heavily accented with the clipped and flipped vowel sounds that indicate a Slavic mother tongue. He extended his hand.

"Nice to meet you, too." We shook. "May I pet your Grim?"

"That's entirely up to them, but it's fine with me." He nodded and smiled.

I leaned toward the shadowy dog, my hand extended at a level with their eyes. I let them sniff and form their own opinion of me. At first, they leaned back, lifting their head to study my face. It was up in the air at that point whether they'd be okay with me.

Ember stirred on my shoulder, lifting her head and extending her long neck to get a good look at the Grim. They locked gazes, and something passed between them that my bond with Ember only let me sense to a small degree.

"Peep." She said this with certainty, for all the world like a person giving a definitive answer to a question I couldn't possibly guess. I mean, what kind of query would a Grim straight out of the Under have for a young dragonet? Apparently an important one.

The Grim looked at me, then stepped forward and did the last thing I expected at that point—they licked my hand. Smiling, I reached out to scratch behind their ears. The tail wag got more intense, to the point where Dr. Brodsky put his hands on his teacup and saucer to keep them from rattling.

"Well, she's certainly got your touch, Mildred." Dr. Liz smiled, showing fangs that were just slightly elongated. That meant she was well-fed, which made sense because the teacup in front of her was half-full of bagged blood.

Bubbe always kept some on hand. Vampirism happened. Any psychic or magus could get turned just like a regular human. She wouldn't turn away a critter in need just because the person with them happened to be undead. As an extraveterinarian, she even had a license to keep stuff like that here in her office. Some magical creatures also drank blood.

As I continued playing with the Grim, moving my scratches from behind the ears to under their chin, I tried to remember where I'd heard the name "Brodsky" before. I couldn't quite put my finger on it, but it seemed familiar, and recent, too. One thing for sure, nobody at school had mentioned him. Maybe on television? Could he have given a Ted Talk on summoning or something?

"Do you need anything, Bubbe?" I stood, stepping back toward the doorway. "I was thinking of heading down to Walgreen's."

I decided that our conversation could wait until her guests had gone. Some of it was sensitive, and critical of the Fairbanks family. They might have been more influential than I imagined. Coincidence was a thing, after all. After the week I had at school, the last thing I wanted to do was tempt it.

"Yes, if you don't mind." She nodded, bustling about with her teacup at the sink. "I'm running low on dish soap." She held up the bottle and shook it, sloshing green sudsy dregs from side to side.

"Okay, I'll be back in about fifteen minutes or so." I waved and smiled. "It was nice to meet you, Dr. Brodsky, and to see you again, Dr. Liz."

"Don't tell me you remember the last time, child." The vampire doctor grinned. "You could barely speak back then."

"All the same, *you* remember it."

Her grin grew into a smile. "Just so. And thank you."

This time, I headed out through the front of the office. There was a back door, but the small fenced yard behind the house was where we exercised the critters who needed it. We had quite the obstacle course back there, mostly for the benefit of four-legged earthbound creatures recovering from sprains or broken limbs.

At the end of the driveway, I glanced up at Izzy's house, which was dark. I should've expected that because she'd already told me it was Parents' Night at Messing Prep. "Parents" in the Mendez family always meant everyone, including Abuela and her grouchy old cat. I grinned as I turned right down Hawthorne Street, picturing Mittens ignoring a gymnasium full of psychics.

Ember hummed softly on my shoulder, contented with the bellyful of pizza and the cool night air. Salem's traffic picked up in September, even though all the big Halloween events were a month out. Folks interested in visiting during the busiest time of year sometimes came up early to familiarize themselves with the general area ahead of time. Others just wanted to see the history and didn't mind missing all the live events, costumes, and carnivals.

As I turned the corner onto Derby Street, I saw a trio of teenagers staring at the wax museum. They were not from Hawthorn Academy since I didn't recognize them. One tapped the others on their shoulders, jerking her chin at me. They whispered, smiled, and cooed, making it clear they'd noticed Ember. Back before the Reveal, kids like me had special amulets to prevent that kind of thing from happening.

It was a freer world now, something I tried not to take for granted.

"Go on, say hi," I murmured.

"Peep!" I felt Ember lift her head off my shoulder, and in my peripheral vision, saw her stretch out her neck as far as it would go as she greeted the mundane kids.

One of the teenagers, clearly my age or even older, clapped her hands. I smiled at them as I went by. It wasn't just me who appreciated this new, open world. Kids like these wouldn't even have believed in magic thirty years ago, or if they had, they would have feared it.

Overall, I thought the world had changed for the better, although vampires and some of the shifters still fought for their rights. That made me wonder again how the brother of someone like my mom, who raised me with this viewpoint, could take the opposite.

Because he's an extramagus like you.

"No." Stupid inside voice. And my protest didn't even work, because it continued.

Yes. Someday you'll be the one watching the world burn.

I shook my head, keeping my mouth shut because I didn't want to frighten my awestruck peers or anyone else on the street. And if that insistent little voice in my head was right, I'd better hold on to that feeling as long as I could—the one where I cared about other people even when they were total strangers.

Ember sensed something wrong. She curled her around my arm, twining it down my bicep, and rubbed her cheek against mine, humming softly. I recognized the tune, the one Bubbe always sang in her office.

"Thanks." This time I didn't keep my voice quiet. Instead, I reached up and scratched her under the chin to make it obvious to any passersby that I was talking to my familiar and not myself. Besides, who could possibly have taken a word of kindness as a threat?

Your magisupremacist uncle, for one.

I sighed, refusing to give in to that line of thinking. Besides, I was at Walgreen's already. Well, across the street from it, anyway. I stood on the sidewalk in front of the crosswalk, waiting for traffic to stop. When it did, I strode along, eyes up and waving at the drivers.

As I stepped inside the drugstore, I realized there wasn't anything I wanted from here. The errand was only a ploy, after all, so I headed down the aisle with household items and grabbed dish soap for Bubbe. I wanted to be convincing, I'd have to pick something for myself as well, so I wandered up and down the aisles, looking at nothing.

Finally, I knew what to do. I strode toward the registers, grabbed a pack of gum, and put it on the counter with the soap. I went through the motions of paying, exchanging common pleasantries with the changeling behind the counter. Yes, she was a changeling, and I knew because her glamour slipped as she helped me.

"Your dragonet's adorable." She smiled, flashing green teeth. In a moment, she covered her mouth with one hand. "Sorry."

"It's okay. I understand."

"You're at the prep school, aren't you?"

"Yeah, but I grew up here in town. Going to hang out with my family off-campus for the weekend." I smiled. "It's kinda nice to be home."

"Oh, that's true. I can't wait until Thanksgiving when I can go back to Fitchburg."

"Are you at Gallows Hill?"

"Yeah, just started. To be honest, I kind of prefer working here?" Her voice lifted at the end of her sentence as though asking me if it was okay to feel that way.

"Hey, my name's Aliyah. Me and my friends know this town, so if you ever have questions, you know, like cool places to visit or spots to escape the tourists, just message me here."

I flipped my receipt over and jotted down my chat handle, then tore the bottom off and pushed it toward her.

"Wow, thanks." She shook her head. "I'm Brianna. It's not easy to make friends around here, and most of the other changelings at school aren't cool with Goblins."

She scribbled her handle down on a section of blank receipt that she got off her register. I took it and smiled, tucking into my pocket.

"I'm not on much during the week because Hawthorn's a no-phone zone." I chuckled. "But I'll probably be here on weekends with friends from town and school."

"That's good to know. The only folks I know here are co-workers. I didn't know Hawthorn had rules against cell service."

"It's just impossible to get a signal on campus. Anyway, one of my friends goes to Gallows Hill and isn't even a changeling. Send me a message tomorrow, okay?"

"I will. Talk to you later!"

I headed out of the store, retracing the route I took there to get back home. The streets had quieted down a bit, and the walk back proceeded without incident. When I arrived at Bubbe's office again, I headed through the front door.

When I got to the kitchen, the guests were gone. My grandmother had tidied up—well, at least as much as she could without dish soap. I fixed that problem for her, taking it from the bag, opening the bottle, and squeezing a dollop onto the sponge she was holding.

"Thanks, Bissell."

I helped, drying the dishes and setting them on the rack. I wasn't sure where she kept the yellow tea set, and I didn't want to go rummaging through her cabinets. I studied the china, certain I'd never seen it used before and wondering why. Perhaps this was just for when Dr. Liz visited, to make the bagged blood more appealing.

When we finished the simple task, Bubbe gestured at the table. I took a seat and she sat in the chair opposite, leaning forward on her elbows. Instead of tea, a tall glass sat on the table between us, beside a spoon on a folded napkin, a can of plain seltzer water, and a bottle of chocolate syrup. She put the spoon in the glass, dumped in some of the syrup, then popped the can and poured the seltzer over it all.

The mixture foamed up, reminding me of the disastrous lab experiment. I closed my eyes and sighed. Would my experiences at Hawthorn Academy ruin even the simple pleasure of sharing an old childhood treat with my grandmother? I hoped not.

"Sha got your smile?"

"I wish it were that simple, Bubbe."

"Everybody says high school's supposed to be the best time of your life. Well, almost everybody. I won't say it, and you won't hear your mother repeat that platitude either. So, what's wrong?"

I explained to her. Not everything, though. Absolutely not about being an extramagus, and I didn't tell her that Noah had turned on me or bring up the rivalry between DeBeer and Luciano. But I mentioned that I was being teased about Richard Hopewell.

Bubbe didn't interrupt. It wasn't her way. She liked to hear the entire story before asking more questions, let alone commenting. I wasn't sure where her patience came from, but it wasn't a trait I inherited, at least not for anyone but magical critters.

That was how I avoided naming names or getting into details about the incidents. She'd heard about the fires in the cafeteria and the lab, and I left the formation of Hal's clique for the end. That way, at least she'd know I'd be okay. After that, I moved right along, changing the subject to Logan's problem.

"So, remember the dragonet you had here in your office? The blue one? Logan painted a picture, and I think that's the critter his parents sent from Vegas with him."

"But Bissell," Bubbe shook her head. "That little fellow's not bonded to anyone."

"Are you sure?" I blinked. "He's supposed to be my friend's familiar."

"I've been in this business for a decade longer than your father has been alive and studied with your great-grandfather in this field for half as long as that to boot. Are you really asking if I'm sure?" The twinkle in her eye and her smirk told me she wasn't angry, just engaging in a little banter.

"Okay. There's more." I took a deep breath before continuing because this was a whammy. "I also think I know the magus who belongs with that dragonet, and it's not the friend I just mentioned."

"It's your fellow, isn't it?"

"Excuse me?" I blinked.

"You know the one. He was around half the summer with Izzy and Cadence."

"Dylan? He's just a friend."

"Well, then your friend fellow." She nodded.

"How did you know I meant him?"

"He's at least as powerful as you are with magic, and dragonets are particular about that sort of thing."

"That can't be right."

"Why?"

"Because he said his parents had him tested and he's average."

"That's nothing. Your tests were average too."

"What? Nobody tested me."

"Your parents didn't, but your grandfather did."

"I didn't know that." I stirred my egg cream absently.

"It was a secret between him and me."

"I thought he was mundane."

"Yes, that he was." She sighed, her eyes focused inward on something buried deep. "But his work was not."

"What did he do?" I knew already, but I thought Bubbe would feel better saying it out loud.

"He was a military doctor who cared for the early extrahuman enlistees." She smiled kindly. "This, of course, was why you were so inspired by that mundane student down at Providence Paranormal."

"He never had the sort of opportunity Lynn Frampton did, and I think it's pretty amazing how times have changed for the better." I closed my eyes, tears threatening a critical breach. "So, how could my own uncle try to murder her?"

"Your grandfather and your uncle never met, but they'd have been enemies if they had. Some see change as a miracle—people like your mother, your father, and I. But others? Well, they see it as a threat."

"I don't understand." I opened my eyes, sniffling. The tears hadn't come yet.

"That's a blessing and a curse, Aliyah. May it prove to be more the former than the latter."

"Speaking of blessings and curses, Bubbe, what we do about the dragonet? No matter what happens, at least one of the guys is going to suffer."

"Any sentient being knows suffering is inevitable, but any healer knows one thing more—suffering ends. I'm proud of you for offering them help. Bring them by sometime this weekend, and we'll see what we can do."

"Thanks, Bubbe. I love you." And there went the waterworks. Tears rolled down my face, dropping to the table, onto my arm, into my egg cream, even on Ember.

"Peep." She rubbed her cheek against mine, not caring that she got all wet.

"I love you too, Bissell."

She said no more that night, but it was more than enough.

CHAPTER NINE

I made my way up the back stairs in the dark. I didn't need light to see. I had used that staircase for sixteen years, practically learned to walk on it. But as I ascended, a pale golden light banished some darkness in front of me. I glowed.

"Go away." I tried shutting off the solar magic, but it was no use. No matter how much I wanted to wish away being an extramagus, the powers I didn't want wouldn't leave me alone.

I stood on the top step, my hand on the doorknob, unable to open the door and enter the apartment. It wasn't that I didn't want to be in there. All I wanted was to go home, and it was right there for me on the other side of the door. All I had to do was turn and push.

But did I have the right? I wasn't the person I had been when I left for Hawthorn Academy. Was this why Noah spent so much time there and seemed so reluctant to leave school? Had he changed too?

No. He was just like Dad, except for being a gay teenager. He even looked like our father when he didn't have time to straighten his hair. My brother was a Morgenstern through and through, down to the serpent familiar, even if he wasn't happy about it.

But I was different. I resembled evil Uncle Richard more than my mother, despite what my family had said my whole life. Were they lying? Did Mom see the brother she'd never mentioned in my face every day? Was I the reason she seemed so tired all the time?

The glow persisted, even growing stronger. I wished I'd never have to see it again, so I closed my eyes and focused, telling it to get lost, scram, beat it, make like a tree and leave. When I opened my eyes, it was still there, like a rotten smell under the sink even after you took the garbage out.

"Just go already!" I didn't know if I spoke to the solar magic or myself at this point, but that time, it worked. The glow vanished.

I almost fell into the apartment as the door was pulled open. Ember stretched her wings out behind me, steadying me.

"Go where?" My father stood blinking into the darkness. "We just got home. Did you want to get some ice cream?"

"Nowhere, Dad. Sorry." I shrugged, stepping through the door and into the space between the kitchen and the dining room. "Sorry."

"Did you get in a fight with your friends?" Dad lifted his glasses, peering closely at me. "Are you okay?"

"No, but school was a whole week of stress."

"Do you need a hug?"

I couldn't say another word or I'd burst into tears, so I flung my arms around my father instead. He hugged back, lifting me off the ground even though I was almost exactly his height. Or maybe a tiny bit taller. This was exactly what I needed.

I couldn't possibly think him even secretly disappointed in me, let alone afraid I'd turn out like his criminal brother-in-law, not after a hug like that.

"Don't forget me."

Mom stood behind Dad, her arms outstretched. He pulled her in for a group hug. I got exactly the same feeling from Mom—that she loved me. Both my parents did, and while I wasn't wrong to question it, I probably wouldn't be making that mistake again anytime soon.

While I moved the laundry from the washer to the dryer, I thanked them for the pizza and told them I'd been to visit Bubbe and that I was tired. I didn't have to feign a yawn as I said good night and headed up the back stairs.

I lucked out in the parental department.

It wasn't until I washed my face, brushed my teeth, and got my pajamafied self into bed that I realized almost none of my school friends shared that luck. But that was a concern for tomorrow. For now, I needed sleep.

I woke to Ember peeping in my face. It wasn't loud, more chirpy and social. She was probably lonely after being at Hawthorn Academy for a whole week, playing with other familiars.

"Don't worry, girl, we'll see another dragonet today."

She flapped her wings, letting out a trilling sound I'd never heard her make before.

"I'll have to ask Bubbe what that means." I sat up, stretching before cautiously making my way out of the bed. The last thing I wanted was a goose egg from the low ceiling to start my day.

Once I'd showered, brushed my teeth, and gotten dressed, I headed downstairs. My laundry was in a basket at the foot of it, so I picked that up and turned back around, putting it on my bed to be folded later. No, I didn't expect my parents to do laundry chores for me, especially not while I slept in. I was just glad they paid the bills.

Down in the kitchen, Dad made pancakes. With blueberries. Ember fluttered down to the counter and started prancing around, peeping and making an epic fuss until Dad reached out and tossed a blueberry in her direction.

Ember had to swoop off the counter and dive in order to catch the fruit before it hit the floor. When she came up, she held the little blueberry in her mouth, facing the shiny glass front of the stove. She must have liked how she looked holding it or something.

I headed to the dining room and set the table except for the plates, which I kept stacked where Dad could reach them. Mom came out of her office to carry each plate to the table once he'd laden it with cakes. I got syrup, cinnamon, butter, and cream out of the kitchen. Once we were seated and half the pancakes were gone, Mom asked about my plans for the day.

"My friends Dylan and Logan are coming from Hawthorn. Logan's coming first, before lunch. Dylan can't make it until later because he works in the café."

"Oh." Mom's smile was unexpected. "I used to work there."

"Really?" I tried not to blink or otherwise seem more than casually curious. I'd have never thought she'd been a work-study student, not with the kind of money the Hopewells came from. I wouldn't have been surprised if she'd said that last week.

"Yes. It's how I met your father. I served him coffee."

"You mean, you spilled on me." He chuckled.

"Well, at least it was iced."

"Doesn't matter. You were still hot."

"Mom! Dad!" I had grown out of thinking boys were icky, but somehow the idea of sex put me off, especially when it involved my parents. "Eww!"

"Aliyah." My mother tilted her head, arching an eyebrow with an expression I recognized as faux-serious. "You and Noah didn't spring fully formed from your father's brow and calf like Athena and Dionysus."

"Still." I shook my head, my expression sobering. I couldn't help it at the mention of my brother, but the rest of the family had no clue about the issues between Noah and me yet.

My parents finished their breakfast with faint grins on their faces. The two of them were still very much in love, although it was a mystery to me how anyone ended up together. Every remotely romantic interaction I'd had was more awkward than a turtle on its back. Maybe someday I'd figure it out. Or maybe not. Izzy didn't seem concerned about it. I wished it didn't bother me.

The doorbell rang as we were rinsing dishes. Mom and Dad finished up, letting me answer it. I opened the door to find Izzy and Cadence. They came in, and we sat on the living room sofa. I sank against the cushions, relieved to be with my most familiar and best friends.

"We're going out." My father poked his head in through from the kitchen. "Bubbe has some critters that need exercise, the kind you walk on a leash, so we're taking a stroll around town. See you girls later!"

We all said goodbye. Cadence grabbed the remote, flipping through channels on the television absently. She usually had to occupy part of her attention with something while trying to focus. I was used to that, although it drove other people up the wall. By other people, I meant all of Izzy's siblings. They didn't have much patience.

"So, what's this big thing that came up?" Cadence didn't look at me, but I knew she was asking because she cared. "The one you wouldn't even talk about over the you-know-what?"

"Remember the explosion in lab I told you about?" They nodded. "Well, it's worse than just property damage because I realized I can do this."

I held out my hand and called up that awful solar magic. Cadence dropped the remote. She leaned over and picked it up again but stared the entire time at the globe of light in my hand. Izzy smacked her face with her palm.

"No way." The mermaid's lips were dry, her voice a parched whisper. She cleared her throat. "No freaking way."

"Yes, way." Izzy held a card in her hand, plucked from the bag slung across her body. "Yes, freaking way."

It was the sun reversed. In case you don't know what that means, just wait. Izzy laid it on me.

"This is some unclear, fake, sad, oppressive shit right here." She slapped the card down on the coffee table, then looked me straight in the eye. "Who's griefing you about being an extramagus?"

"I already told you. Some upperclassman named Charity Fairbanks, even though she doesn't know for sure." I swallowed past the lump in my throat. "And someone else who's even worse."

"Stop acting like this cryptic-ass card, Aliyah, and tell us the whole story."

I didn't have to hide this from my friends like with my family. They weren't related to Noah, and they didn't even like him that much, so I told them all of it, down to how he ignored me. I even mentioned the unspoken detail that had disturbed me for the entire week.

"I was in the infirmary twice, and he didn't even visit."

"Wow, what a jerk." Cadence shook her head. "I can't believe I almost set him up with my neighbor. Shelby dodged a bullet right there."

"Mean people suck." Izzy frowned.

"You guys want coffee?" I stood up, rubbing my hands against my legs where my elbows had pressed too hard on my thighs. "My folks will be back any minute, and I don't want them to know all of this."

"Coffee sounds great." Izzy nodded, swiping her card off the table and tucking it back in her bag. "Should we go now?"

"Okay, but we might go back again after Logan gets here."

"Is that your non-Dylan classmate?" Cadence stood up, fluffing her hair. "Is he cute?"

"You'll figure it out, Cadence." I stepped toward the door, grabbing my knapsack off the hook. "Oh, wait."

My friends waited by the door as I left a brief note for my parents, telling them I'd be out. They did the same for me, and I didn't want them to worry. I also grabbed my phone off the charger, checking it first to see if Brianna from Walgreens had sent me a message. There was nothing, so I just brought it along.

We headed down the stairs and out into the sunlit day. It was the best kind you could get in early autumn, where the light fell through just enough cloud cover to look dreamy and the breeze only just barely nipped. We headed around the corner and down Essex Street, taking our time. We all knew where we were going and how to get there since there was only one place extrahumans our age went for coffee.

The Witch's Brew wasn't technically on Essex Street, or any other for that matter. Instead, the front door was in an alcove. We pushed through the door with its weathered wood and cauldron-shaped stained glass, stepping into a space steeped in the warm aroma of freshly ground coffee.

This place didn't heal all the sore spots inflicted by my week at Hawthorn Academy, but it came close.

We waited in the short line, then ordered beverages. The enormous ornate mural clock on the wall had the broomstick halfway between eleven and twelve, with the wand just a hair off noon. The hour and the nice weather were two reasons we took our drinks outside. The third, of course, was that we had to search for the door to my school to meet Logan on his way out.

Essex Street was about as busy as it got on a day outside October. Most of the tourists walked with food or drinks instead of sitting inside, for one thing. That was probably why the tricycle-powered Polaroid cart almost ran us over, but it swerved out of the way just in time before screeching to a halt.

"Not again." Izzy rolled her eyes.

"Uh-oh." Cadence put one hand to her cheek.

"Hi." I stepped in the way as the camera dude hopped off and jogged over. "We're okay but running a little late, so no time to talk, Azrael."

"Are you sure?" He peered past me at Izzy with stars in his eyes. He didn't even notice Ember peeping curiously at him. She'd never met this fixture of Essex Street atmosphere yet.

I mentioned before that Isabella Mendez isn't interested in boys, and probably not girls either. Azrael Ambersmith was the main reason I was sure this is true. He was a Goblin changeling, the youngest member of a family otherwise made up of magi and psychics, and he'd been crushing on Izzy since second grade. He was also almost as pretty as Logan, but in a shabbier steampunk sort of way.

His name sounded like it came from the pages of an old pulp fantasy novel from the 1960s. Maybe it did, for all I knew. The Ambersmiths were the local magipsychic crafters, tinkers, and second-hand item dealers. Certainly, they'd read some of the books lining the walls of their storefront farther down the block.

Plenty of people's trash got turned into treasures in their work-shops and sold from one of their storefronts or this cart. Azrael's aunt had married the cobbler, too. Ambersmiths were all over the wi-fi-negating zone around Hawthorn Academy, and by all appearances, they made a decent living because of it. The Polaroid cart had plenty of customers once folks realized they couldn't reliably use their phones to take pictures here.

"I'm meeting a friend from Hawthorn, Az." Out of the three of us, I had remained on the best terms with Azrael since the end of elementary school. That was why, whenever he came around, they left deflecting him to me. At least this time, I didn't feel like I had to lie.

"Oooh, I know where the door is today! Just saw someone come out of it, in fact."

"Thanks, Az." I grinned.

"I'll just hop on the trike and lead the way." He jogged back to his ride, and I followed.

"Whatever." Izzy followed too, staring at the cobblestones.

"At least he's nice to look at, Iz."

"I don't care about that stuff, Cadence." Izzy shook her head. "Flowers are pretty, too."

"Well, think of him like a painting or statue or something, then."

"Not helping."

"Sorry." Cadence twirled a lock of her hair between her fingers. Suddenly, she stopped cold. "He didn't ever do...anything? Like, improper?"

"No. I just don't want to date people." Izzy shrugged.

"Okay. Because I was gonna say, if he did do anything—"

"Thanks, Cadence." Izzy finally looked up. "You're a good friend."

"Hey, what's with the cat?" I pointed.

They looked in the direction I indicated and saw it too-a scruffy stray cat. Well, she was only scruffy because her long hair was all matted. Also, she seemed awfully underfed. I was about to call out to her, thinking maybe Bubbe could help. Even if she was mundane, food was food. But Azrael rang the bell on his handlebars and stopped his cart. He jerked his thumb at what was usually an old boarded up door. I knew better, of course.

Az took one last long look at Izzy before ringing his bell again and taking off down the street. I looked around for the cat again but didn't see her.

Just then, the door opened and Logan walked out. He noticed us right away. We were super-hard to miss, standing right in his way like that. It only took him three steps to cross the distance. That was when I realized why I felt so awkward around him.

Logan Pierce looked at me the same way Azrael Ambersmith looked at Izzy.

And I'd thought I was so slick, noticing Grace's crush on Dylan. Of course, Cadence saw it right away. I was surprised she didn't whip out a wedding planner instead of just elbowing me in the ribs.

Before my merfriend could say anything, I introduced Logan to everybody, then invited him down to visit Bubbe. It was a short enough walk to pass the time in conversation with basics about Logan's life outside of school. He had ready answers for questions like that, although I wondered how many were well-rehearsed and designed to please his parents.

By the time we turned on Hawthorne Street, I realized the cat had come back. She trotted to keep up, but only because she was so worn out. I saw her stop before Izzy's house, dropping to the sidewalk too suddenly.

"Just a sec, guys. Animal in trouble here."

I turned back for the poor kitty. She was on her side, panting heavily, almost like a dog. Logan hovered, peering over my shoulder.

"Peep?" Ember fluttered down, landing on the sidewalk. Once there, she sat back on her haunches, lifting her head straight up in the air and letting out a long, keening wail.

"Easy, girl," I said to both critters. "I'm gonna help. See?"

Bending down was easy, scooping the cat up too much so. She was very light, like the wind could have carried her away with ease. I got the impression of a dried-out husk, but she was cool to the touch, not hot like an animal fighting an illness.

"Just around the corner and into a building, okay? Then you'll have a chance to get well."

Izzy and Cadence knew better than to get in my way in situations like these. Logan, not so much, or maybe he was just as concerned about the unfortunate stray. At any rate, he followed closely. And for once, he didn't stare at me. He only had eyes for the cat.

I thought back to Familiar Studies and how he always played with the polydactyl. And then that the possum tried bonding with him twice. At that moment, I understood the shortcomings of that entire series of lessons. They don't do what they were designed for—helping magi without familiars meet suitable companions.

For some people, only crisis could create enough vulnerability to bond with a magical creature. I should know since it happened that way for me. Why not Logan? But I had to hope this kitty was more than she seemed to be because if not, Logan's need to appease his family might lead to rejection. In this state, that could kill her.

The moment we got inside, Bubbe came out from behind the counter. She took charge immediately, rushing the cat back into a room—the one right across from the blue dragonet's, in fact. Logan glanced over his shoulder, directly at the half-open door where the blue-scaled beauty strutted.

He turned his back on the dragonet without hesitation, following Bubbe and the cat into the empty treatment room. His shoulders were square, his jaw set, but both trembled.

We all watched, silent and barely breathing as my grandmother worked. She managed to revive the cat, or at least her paws stirred, and she opened her eyes.

"Peep?" Ember perched on top of the lamp in the corner, casting a winged shadow. She blinked, tilting her head one way and then the other, but she didn't keen again. Considering that dragonets only do that while mourning death, that was a good sign.

"Cadence, fetch me some water, please."

"I'll do it, Bubbe."

"No. You shouldn't touch any of the things we'll use for her at this point. She can't handle any more fire energy in this state, Bissel."

"I'm water." Logan stepped forward. "I mean, I'm a magus, and it's my element."

"Well then, no need to fetch a basin." Bubbe gave him a faint smile.

"Please conjure an orb for me. They've taught you that much at Hawthorn by now, yes?"

"Yes, ma'am." He held his hands at his middle, one over the other like in Gym for Bishop's Row. The space between his hands filled rapidly, and without needing to be told, he walked up to the table like he'd been doing this all his life.

"Now drop it all right on her."

"What?"

"Won't she drown?"

"Who does that to a cat?"

All those questions came from us, not Logan. He followed orders, drenching the poor critter on the table.

The next thing I knew, Ember swooped in arcs overhead, singing happily. The cat sat up, her fur clinging to her sides. It was still matted and bedraggled, but her eyes were brighter. The warm, soothing sound of her purr filled the room. She curled up in a cozy ball, gazing up at the boy who'd saved her until he glanced down and their eyes met.

Logan's entire face lit up. I'd seen that exactly once before, when Noah bonded with Lotan, and that moment had been fleeting. This one was sustained, so grounds for doubt remained, but mostly I recognized the truth because I'd had the feeling behind his expression myself.

The day I met Ember.

Logan's familiar troubles were far from over because of his parents, but at least he could stay on the Familiars track at Hawthorn. I watched him approach the table to stroke the cat's flank. When he pulled his hand up, a matted clump of fur came with it. He blinked for a moment, then grinned.

"A mercat." Logan shook the shed fur off his hand, tossing it in the trash. "I can't believe it."

"Yes, and it's a miracle you found her in time. I've never seen one this dehydrated in all my years as an extraveterinarian." Bubbe handed him a brush with rounded bristles.

"Well, she doesn't have to worry about that anymore." He went to work, pulling the bristles gently along her sides. She turned so he could reach more of the matts.

He brushed them out, and not the same way as with a regular cat, either. Mercats only got like this if they spent too much time without a bath. Like Cadence, they could walk on land, but in saltwater, they had fins and a tail from the midsection down. Unlike merfolk, who could go years without setting foot in the ocean, the cats needed a good drenching every few days. She must have been out on the street for a week with no rain. Bubbe was right—we did find her just in time.

It wasn't a miracle, though. Finding the cat at the same time Logan came out of the school smacked of coincidence. That was just fate for extrahumans.

CHAPTER TEN

We all sat in Bubbe's kitchen, chatting as the mercat rested in the other room. Bubbe set out a basin of salted water for her to climb into as needed, but the best thing to help her recover was rest.

"What's her name, Logan?"

"Uh, I'm not sure."

"Oh?" Bubbe raised an eyebrow.

"Yeah. It's not like I bonded with her or anything." He sat up straighter as though remembering something. "I almost forgot to mention, Doctor Morgenstern. I came to find my—"

Just then, Bubbe tapped her earring. I knew what that meant.

"Someone's in the lobby. Hang on a moment." She rose and headed out.

We all heard the murmur of voices out there. And of course, everyone recognized the new one. Dylan arrived early. He followed Bubbe in and leaned against the wall because we'd run out of chairs.

"They let me out of work because I got deliveries done so fast." He grinned at Cadence and Izzy. "Good to see you two ladies again."

Everybody said hello, the girls getting up to give Dylan hugs. Of course, I'd just seen him the day before, so I didn't bother. Logan didn't either, but he did stand up to share a handshake.

"You were saying, Logan?"

"Yeah, I'm here for my dragonet. Well, technically he's my parent's, but they sent him here with me, so he's my responsibility." He pulled his painting from the tube slung over his shoulder. "That's him."

"That's a handsome little fellow, and yes, he's here, although I'm not sure he'll be happy to see you, Logan." Bubbe raised her eyebrow. She'd seen him turn away from the dragonet then, just like I had.

Dylan's mouth dropped open. He closed it before Logan, Izzy, or Cadence noticed, but I did. Ember too. She fluttered off my shoulder and over to Dylan's, rubbing her head against the side of his head, tousling his hair.

"What's up with that?" Izzy pointed, blinking at my dragonet's disloyal behavior.

"I don't know?" I slumped against the back of my chair. "She's never done that before. Bubbe?"

"Hmmm." My grandmother sighs. "I think it's time you all met our scaly runaway. Come along, everyone."

She led us down the hall toward the back of the office. The last room on the left was unoccupied and clean. Bubbe asked us to wait there, then left, heading back toward the blue dragonet's room. She returned in moments with the creature in her arms.

"So, here's the little man of the hour."

Logan was about to speak, but the dragonet cut him off. Instead of peeping like Ember he had a chirping voice. He clearly had no regard for the magus he'd come to Salem with, either. In fact, he squirmed madly, trying to get out of Bubbe's arms so frantically I was worried he'd scratch her.

Before anything like that happened, my grandmother let go. She was a good doctor and has developed a way with just about every type of magical creature over years of practice. It might not even be mysterious to her why Logan's parents would try to pair him with a dragonet that wasn't even representative of his water element. But then again, it was her business to understand magical creatures, not the minds of magi in showbiz.

The dragonet flew up and down the hall a few times, flitting past the doorway as we watched him. He shimmered in the lights of the hallway, clearly frustrated that this wasn't open sky. Air creatures were like that. Coop them up for too long, and they got downright hyperactive.

After three laps, he divebombed Dylan.

Ember leaped off his shoulder, getting out of the way but leaving Dylan off balance. That was why he tumbled to the floor, nearly as tangled with the dragonet as I had been with my own the day she'd found me.

Moments later, their eyes met. It was just like what happened between the mercat and Logan in the other room, but of course, Dylan had no reservations about this occasion, unlike his roommate. Or at least he was free of them at the moment.

"His name is Gale."

"Oh, no." Logan crossed his arms on the examination table and leaned forward, burying his face in his arms. "My parents—"

"Sorry, Logan." Dylan looked up from the floor, eyes wide and face slack. "Didn't mean it."

"Yeah, it just happened." His voice was muffled, hard to hear the tone in it, but I caught the hitch between words—trying not to cry. "I get it."

Bubbe was like someone watching a ping-pong match. Her eyes moved from the boy by the table to the boy on the floor, her face as still as stone. She grew up at a time where all magic, including bonding with familiars, was totally secret. From her perspective, an unbonded familiar could choose any magus. Maybe she didn't automatically understand what was wrong here, so I decided to explain, but not with everybody just sitting here. This was Logan's business, though clearly, he shared it with Dylan too. But not Izzy and Cadence. He'd just met them.

"Hey, girls?" I stood up. "I was thinking we ought to go for pizza, but considering everything that just happened here, we need takeout."

"Sure, we'll pick it up." Izzy grabbed Cadence by the shoulder, shaking her. "I'm short on cash, though."

"Here you go." I dug in my knapsack, took out my wallet, and got the money Mom and Dad had left for me this morning. I handed that to Izzy. "I think we'll need more than one pie."

"Yeah, I remember how much Dylan the bottomless pit eats." She chuckled. "Come on, Cadence. You have to help me carry pizzas because I'm not gonna be able to bring that many myself."

"Thanks, Izzy."

Having a psychic friend insured that she always got it when you couldn't say what you meant. I missed her so much at school. My friends from town headed out, leaving me alone with Bubbe and the boys. Once I heard the door between the clinic and the waiting room close, I explained.

"Logan's parents wanted him to bond with a dragonet, and Dylan's parents left it up to him to find a familiar on his own." I sighed. "I know this is super-complicated and not what you're used to dealing with. Honestly, I didn't think it would go this way myself, or at least, I'd hoped it would be better. I'm sorry, you guys."

"It's not your fault." Logan looked up, his eyes rimmed with red and his face tear-stained. "It's mine."

"You bet your bottom dollar it's not." Bubbe crossed her arms over her chest, her expression sterner than I'd ever seen it. "This is on your parents. I've never heard of such a thing, trying to force a bond. Who do they think they are?"

"You haven't heard of the Magical Menagerie? I mean, it's on TV and everything." Logan shook his head. "That's my parents. Or it might as well be, because as far as they're concerned, the show is their life. It's supposed to be mine and my sister's too."

"Noah never said anything about Elanor going through anything like this."

"That's because my sister bonded immediately with the firebird they picked for her. The creatures they keep around never want anything to do with me, and they never let me near more understated critters. They say those won't look good on the show. It's all my fault. There must be something wrong with me."

"I may have just met you today, young man, but that's absolutely incorrect." Bubbe stepped across the room, placing her hand on

Logan's shoulder. "The empathy and concern you showed earlier indicates you're a good lad with his priorities straight. You saved that mercat just in time."

"Mercat? Did you seriously rescue one? That's awesome!" Dylan tried to coax Gale out of his shirt. "Come on, dude, get out of there."

"Yeah, her name is Doris." He scratched his thumb again, mangling the cuticle and the nail this time.

"So, you did bond with her." I sighed, trying to muster some form of consolation for my friend. It was what Bubbe would do, after all. "Logan—"

"My parents are gonna kill me for this. Me and Doris will never look right."

"If they so much as try to harm a hair on your head, Logan Pierce, you come straight to me." Bubbe's color heightened, her eyes bright with righteous anger, her hands aglow.

I never thought I'd see my grandmother like this—fierce and protective. My whole life, she'd been solid and caring like a rock, and here she was, acting like...well, like me in the cafeteria.

"Wow." Dylan gazed at her, then at me. Even Gale stopped to stare.

"Do you really mean that, ma'am?" Logan put his hands flat on the table.

"I protected other students from your school years ago, and I told your headmaster I'd do it again if it ever came to that."

I didn't dare ask what she meant by that or bother clarifying that there was a new Hawkins in charge at Hawthorn Academy this year. She'd given my friend a choice, same as she'd do with a critter in need.

"Thanks, Doctor Morgenstern." Logan straightened up, pulling down the hem of his shirt. "If you don't mind, I'd like to go check on Doris now."

"Come along, then."

Bubbe led the way out the door and down the hall. As I followed, my phone beeped. It was Brianna from Walgreens. I showed Bubbe the message and explained. Once I had permission, I invited her over to have pizza with the rest of us.

As we walked toward Doris' room, Dylan grabbed my hand. I

stopped and turned, blinking at him since that was the last thing in the world I would have expected. We stood there staring at each other until Bubbe's and Logan's voices started up again, crooning at Doris and chatting about her care.

"What's up, Dylan?"

"I didn't want to say this in front of your grandma or act like my problems are worse than Logan's, because they're not. But—"

"Look, your problems are valid, and I already said you could talk to me."

"Okay." He nodded. "Remember when I said they had me tested? For magic ability?"

"Yeah. You said it was average, right?"

"Yeah, but well." He pointed at his midsection, where Gale had wrapped himself, clinging to Dylan's belt with his claws. "How?"

"I mean, he's an air dragonet, and you're an air magus?"

"That part makes sense, but don't they need to bond before they reach a certain age or something?" He scratched his head. "And aren't I going to have trouble? He's not exactly docile. I'm worried I'm not strong enough to work with him."

"You were there the day I met Ember." I arched an eyebrow. "Did I control her then?"

"She got caught in your hair." He smirked. "And no, you didn't."

"Opposite of docile." I grinned. "And then she got hurt, which sort of forced her to chill out. But I think that would have happened eventually anyway, so maybe give it time?"

"I don't have much of that. Gotta go back to work. Most of my hours are on the weekends. What if he flies off into a no familiars area and I'm not strong enough to stop him? Or something? I need the work-study, or I'll have to drop out and go home."

"I can't say I know what it's like, working through school, but you're not alone. You'll meet someone in a little while who's in the same boat. Anyway, as far as training your dragonet, it's got nothing to do with magic."

"Really?"

"It's all about caring, which you're good at. The whole magic power thing is just what gets their attention in the first place, and Bubbe says those early tests aren't too accurate."

"So, all I have to do is care?"

"Help Gale. Play with him, give him affection. Let him pretend to be a wardrobe accessory." I pointed at Ember, who was dozing on my shoulders. "Half the time she thinks she's a scarf. Let him be a belt or whatever."

"Okay, I'll try it." Dylan let go of my hand, then used it to pat Gale on the head. "We're gonna be friends, okay?"

"Cheep," said Gale. Or at least, that was the closest approximation to the sound he made.

"Do you wanna meet a mercat? We can watch her get a bath."

"Okay."

We made it down the hall finally, peering over the half-closed door. Logan was in there with Doris on his lap. Bubbe put the collar that used to be around Gale's neck on Doris', their magic mingling as she helped the pair with that last formality to make their bond official.

As she straightened, we saw the mercat fall asleep. Logan stroked her back with the brush. Most of the matted fur had come away, revealing her actual coat. Instead of dull gray, Doris's flanks looked something like a cross between a tabby and a seal. Her markings were silver with shimmering blue stripes that almost looked like scales.

"Woah, Logan." Dylan whistled. "She's adorable."

"Yeah, she's awesome. But I'm totally biased, and my parents aren't gonna agree." Logan sighed. "Cute's not enough for them."

"Hey, but at least we get to stay in the Familiar program at Hawthorn."

"Good point."

"Do you want help with Gale's collar, Dylan?" Bubbe asked. "Even if we don't get to that today, I can still write all the familiar license paperwork up before you two go back to campus later."

"Um, I don't—"

Bubbe's earring went off again. The aroma of pizza wafted under the door to the back of the office.

"We'll have to wait for now." She opened the door to let Izzy, Cadence, and Brianna in.

Cadence chattered at Brianna in a run-on sentence about the new changeling Bishop's Row team and how she ought to go out for it. Brianna smiled, at ease enough that her glamour totally covered her faerie traits. That was a big difference in demeanor from the stressed-out girl I'd met at Walgreens the night before.

So, I guessed I had met my good deed quota for the day. I smiled as we all headed back to the kitchen to pig out on pizza. Bubbe made her rounds, leaving us to our social time. Logan was quiet, but my friends from town probably thought that was because he held the sleeping Doris in his lap. Only Dylan and I knew better. Logan Pierce just wasn't a social creature.

Dylan was another story. He spun a yarn about some interaction he'd had, working in the café. Somehow, he effortlessly made it sound larger than life. He was in his element here, interacting with a group of people his own age. Most anyone would think all his problems were solved.

The boys went back to campus after finishing their pizza, when Bubbe's signatures on their familiar licenses were dry. Trouble still loomed on the horizon for those two, but it was distant for now.

CHAPTER ELEVEN

I spent the rest of Saturday at Izzy's with Cadence, binging last year's *Ultimate Shifter League* on StreamFlix. We always had a blast doing that because there was something for each of us in it. Cadence, of course, drooled over all the shiny abs on the men. Izzy loved flipping a card or two, trying to predict heel turns and rivalries, and I appreciated the athleticism in all the moves, even if, in reality, they were more acrobatic and choreographed than other sports like Bishop's Row.

We stayed there until well after midnight, not realizing how late it was. Izzy's mom called Cadence a Swyft ride back to her house. Even though Salem wasn't a rough neighborhood, Mrs. Mendez was a divination psychic just like Izzy, so we never questioned her caution. If she'd thought it was safe, she wouldn't have bothered with the car.

On Sunday morning, I slept in. Hal wasn't due to come over until noon, so why was Ember peeping in my ear like the world's scaliest alarm clock? And why was it always so hard to wake up as a bona fide teenager? Ugh.

I sat up, feeling the indent on my cheek where my face had pressed against the seam on my pillowcase. The sheets and blanket were twisted. My pajamas, too. And my hair—some of it stood on end like I'd slept with a small critter trying to burrow into it.

"Ember?" I turned my head, blinking at the dragonet perched on the headboard. She looked awfully disheveled. "Did you do this?"

"Peep." She hung her head.

"Well, there's nothing to do but go in the bathroom and fix it, right?"

"Aliyah!" Dad's voice called up from the bottom of the stairs. "Your friends are here!"

"Crap!" I bolted out of bed, smacking my forehead on the low ceiling. But I had to keep moving.

In the bathroom, I splashed water on my face, rubbing that indented cheek. It was no use, so I moved on to my hair. A bottle of spray conditioner and the old detangling brush Mom had used on me in elementary school made quick work of the bird's nest. After that, I put it up and hopped in the shower. Thank goodness Noah always took forever to get cleaned up. Otherwise, I wouldn't have had this much practice at the sixty-second wash-down.

After tossing my pajamas down the laundry chute, I wrapped the towel around myself. There was a basket of clean laundry in the hall, with some t-shirts on top. I snagged a black one and dashed into my room, where I paired it with some hounds-tooth leggings, maybe too hastily. I didn't realize that until making it down to the first floor, skidding to a stop in front of the dining room table, where Hal sat with Lee and Grace.

"Interesting," Lee tilted his head, peering at the shirt. The left side of his mouth tilted up.

"Woah." Hal blinked. "Probably not a good idea to wear that one back to school."

"I don't know." Grace shrugged. "I totally agree with the sentiment, but you're probably right. It's pretty controversial there."

"Huh?" I tugged the hem of the mysterious shirt, reading upside-down.

Vamp Rights Are Extrahuman Rights

"Oh." Well, at least they hadn't seen the state of my hair or the seam line on my face. "Yeah, this isn't my shirt."

"No?"

"No." I shook my head. "It's...well it *was* Noah's. I thought he tossed it in the donations bag over the summer, though."

"He did, but I took it out and washed it." Dad came in from the kitchen carrying a pitcher of lemonade, his other arm laden with a tray of hamantaschen. "Here are some snacks for you."

"Wow, thanks, Mr. Morgenstern!" Grace popped out of her seat, pacing toward him. "Do you want help carrying those?"

"Thanks, Grace. And you can call me Aaron."

"Those cookies look amazing." Lee smiled. "Did you make them yourself?"

"No. My mother did."

"Oh, Dad never told me Dr. Mildred was a baker." Hal shook his head. "You learn something new every day."

"Your father wouldn't have known, but your grandfather certainly did." Dad chuckled. "Do you know she almost burned down the cafeteria kitchen, trying to bake kosher treats in the middle of the night?"

My classmates responded with gleeful awe. I tried to join in with their mirth, but it felt fake. Bubbe had done all kinds of wild and crazy things and never told me about them.

I noticed Grace stealing a few of the cookies, taking extra and tucking them into the satchel still on her shoulder. Lune sat on his haunches near her, ears up, on alert.

Seeing my roommate outside of school and in my house drove something home. I still thought of her the same way as before—sort of a rebel. But maybe there was a reason, something I couldn't imagine, let alone understand.

Before I could make an excuse to take Grace aside and offer cookies to go, the doorbell rang. I got up and ran to let Izzy and Cadence in.

As they joined the fun, I headed into the kitchen, where I still heard all of them gabbing away. Bubbe must have been baking all week, practically. This made sense because business slowed once Hawthorn started each year. Almost nobody needed educational familiar licenses after that. It didn't pick up again until the middle of

October, when the Halloween tourist season increased the number of extraveterinary emergencies.

I filled a tin with hamantaschen to bring back to school. As I stacked the cookies, Hal came around the counter. Nin dashed down his arm, skidding slightly on the granite as she swiped at a crumb.

"Here, have this." Hal placed his half-eaten treat in front of her and the Pharaoh's Rat picked it up, munching contentedly. "But don't say I didn't warn you about getting a tummy ache later, Nin."

"She's been awfully peckish lately." I grinned at the little critter.

"Yeah, but it's typical for her species. They get a little ravenous in the fall and spring." He reached out to give her a pat on the back.

"A little?" I blinked. "If you don't keep them well-fed, even properly socialized and domesticated Pharaoh's Rats can go feral."

"Yeah, okay. I made a pretty big understatement there." Hal stared at the counter. This topic was not a good look on him.

"So, where's Faith?" I changed the subject.

"Oh, I looked everywhere for her this morning." He sighed. "Told her last night I was going into town and everything, asked if she wanted to come along, and she said maybe. But then, this morning I couldn't find her before we had to leave."

"I'm sure you'll see her later."

"By the way, thanks for inviting us." He grinned. "Everybody's having fun."

"Yeah. Like most of yesterday."

"I heard there were a few hiccups, though?"

"I'd tell you more, but I think that's for Dylan and Logan to do."

"Understood." He nodded. "I saw them come in yesterday after dinner, though. With a mercat and a dragonet."

"You're sort of a gossip, Hal. You know that, right?"

"Yeah. Nobody's perfect."

"Peep!" Ember swooped down from the top of the fridge, holding another empty tin.

"Clearly, she wants me to pack more treats."

"Well, I'll leave you to it, then." Nin dashed across the counter and then up his arm.

As he headed back to the dining room, I considered his familiar. She was friendly and cute, but all the same, Nin belonged to the same species of critter that had murdered an immortal air dragon down in Newport, Rhode Island. Hal would be responsible with her, but people could get scared. The critters were all over the news because of Richard Hopewell's criminal trial. Pharaoh's Rats were rare on this continent. Pretty much the only people who had access to them were Hal's relatives.

Was that why Hal's father was headmaster now instead of his grandpa?

"Ember, can you get my phone, please?"

"Peep." She took off from the counter, speeding toward the stairs on golden wings. In moments, she returned with the device.

I tapped the news app and searched Rhode Island—and there it was. An article about a subpoena over the summer for one Headmaster Hiram Hawkins, which he'd defied. The next article I read said he was detained by state law enforcement and awaiting his trial for contempt. There was nothing else about the connection, but it was obvious why they went after him. The simplest explanation was usually correct.

The critter that had somehow ended up in the Harcourt hoard had come from here. From the Hawkins family.

The one thing I couldn't glean from any of these articles was how, although there were opinion pieces that speculated magical lamp involvement. Until the trial progressed next year, I wouldn't know, so there was no use worrying about it. All the bad guys were locked up, right?

I came around the corner toward the dining room again, and we prepared to head into town. I watched Hal, thinking about how someone from his family was in trouble because my uncle had gone on a rampage a couple of years back.

Or maybe there's actual guilt and corruption in that family.

Yesterday, I'd have told that little voice to shut up. Today, it made a sick sort of sense.

I'd have gone downstairs and asked Bubbe to get real with me about the Morgenstern connection with the Hawkins family because it's there. They'd built the school and this house, while we'd brought in all the magipsychic light and sound.

But there was no time. My friends were waiting for me, and I was sixteen. At that age, people like me were supposed to be out doing fun teenage things, not following some obscure theory about crime and magical families.

I took a moment to dash upstairs and change my shirt, though, because knowing me, I'd only forget to do it later and end up wearing it to school, where I needed to keep my head down.

But I kept the tee. In fact, I wrapped it around the communication orb so it'd be with me at school, even if I didn't wear it there. I wanted it as a reminder, so I didn't forget who I was—a girl who believed in equal rights for all beings. Maybe it'd do my brother some good, too, because he was the one who'd bought this shirt in the first place.

Once upon a time, this sentiment had been Noah's, too. He'd decided to set it aside, leave it at home, forget about it. He wasn't talking about whether he'd lost faith or just felt safer hiding, but he wasn't an extramagus.

The stronger my magics got, the more I'd need reminders like this one.

Out in town, we ambled, letting Lee and Grace take the lead in exploring. Neither of them had spent much time here, and part of the fun in downtown Salem was wandering around to see everything.

Grace noticed The Witch's Brew, and for the only time that day, Lee disagreed about going in with a wrinkle of his nose. He waited outside, and I stayed with him. Cadence and Izzy knew what I liked from there, so I handed them a couple of dollars.

"Thanks, Aliyah."

"No problem. I've been in there about a million times, anyway."

"Scratch doesn't much like the smell of coffee. I'm not sure why."

"I get it. Ember can't stand peanut butter."

"They sure are finicky sometimes, huh?"

"Yeah."

We chattered on, trying to anticipate what we'd learn over the rest of the semester. Impossible, of course. If we already knew that, there'd be no point in going to school.

After a few hours during which we wandered up to the Willows and then all the way down to Salem Pioneer Village in Forest Park, the sunlight went amber and gold. It was late afternoon and time to head back. Grace, Hal, Lee, and I collected our familiars, each of us sorry they couldn't play outside together for a while longer.

We walked up Lafayette Street, cutting through Lafayette Park to get to Washington Street. That led us directly back to Essex, with little on the way besides chain stores and sit-down restaurants we'd see another time.

The door to Hawthorn Academy was next to a dental office. I waved goodbye to my friends, telling them I'd see them later. I wasn't going back without my knapsack and communication orb. More importantly, I wanted to talk to Cadence and Izzy in person one more time before leaving them in Salem for another week.

"I like your friend Lee."

I stopped in the middle of Essex Street, staring at Izzy. Cadence actually squeed, jumping up and down. My psychic friend's reaction to all this fuss was an eye roll and a forehead smack.

"Not like that. Seriously."

Izzy didn't even blush. Cadence pouted. I nodded my head.

"Okay," I said because somebody had to break that silence.

"I'm just saying I think, out of the lot of the Hawthornites, he's got his head on straight. So, if you're looking for some truth in that place, go to him."

"Not Hal?"

"I mean, he's okay, but that kid is definitely hiding something." Izzy shrugged.

"Yeah, Aliyah." Cadence agreed. "I don't think he looks old enough to be there. Is his birthday this week or something, or did he spend like a year in the Under?"

"You know what, I don't know." I chewed my bottom lip and started walking again. "But Hal does. Always seems to have unexpected information, and be in the right place at the right time. I'd think he had a psychic power if I didn't know any better."

That was because an extrahuman could either be psychic or magical but not both. Getting turned into a vampire, becoming a changeling, or picking up a magical shifter item could happen to anyone, but magi and psychics were born without overlap.

"Maybe he's got a device." Izzy shrugged. "But if it's not that, I'm not sure he can be trusted."

"Have you guys been watching the news out of Providence?"

They both nodded, so I let them in on my conspiracy theory about Hal's grandpa being in jail and the Pharaoh's Rats. I was surprised when Cadence added to it.

"Did you hear about his mother?"

"Wait, what?"

"She's from Rhode Island, I heard. There's a rumor that the reason she and his dad split up was because he caught her checking out some man from there. A vampire."

"Where are you getting this?" Izzy blinked.

"The social papers." Cadence chuckled. "You know my mom loves that gossip-column stuff. Whenever I'm bored at home, I pick it up to have a laugh. Apparently, Hal's dad is considered one of the North Shore's most eligible extrahuman bachelors."

"Huh." I snorted. "I had no idea."

I made a mental note to keep an eye on the Hawkins family. Rhode Island was where my uncle had done most of his dirty deeds, and if one or more of them had helped him, I ought to know. But I had less than an hour left with my best friends, so I set all that aside to make the most of that time, having fun together in one of the most magical towns on Earth.

CHAPTER TWELVE

Back in school on Monday, things started feeling normal, finally. Breakfast was uneventful, continuing with the trend late last week of Charity just rolling her eyes, pointing, and occasionally glaring in my general direction.

Despite the fact that I'd been gone for a couple of days, it almost felt like I'd never left. The main difference this week had more to do with Dylan and Logan having familiars, and that they'd gotten them while visiting me.

Doris and Gale fit in nicely with the rest of our group's critters. Gale spent a good deal of his time strutting whenever Ember was nearby. He had a habit of perching on anything high up, fortunately not items or surfaces where familiars weren't allowed. Dylan didn't have much trouble handling him, either, so his worry about controlling his critter got set aside.

Gale was just as much of a ham as his human companion. Whenever Dylan asked him to do something, no matter how nicely, the dragonet made a big show of completing the task like it was a performance. For whatever reason, he put on the appearance of defiance, although he never quite crossed the line into disobedience.

Curious about that, I went out of my way to visit the library and renew my books on dragonets for another week. The Ashfords helped with this. I even asked if they'd seen behavior like that from dragonets before. They told me no, but said they would look into it. It made me wonder what resources the librarians had that students didn't. Perhaps there was an entire second library just for faculty and staff. I wouldn't know unless I decided to teach here someday.

Speaking of teaching, our lessons went fairly well in Professor Luciano's class. He gave us few assignments, although they required a good deal of focus and attention to complete. In the lab, he had us doing safer experiments with stabler substances than on the first day. Anything we needed to infuse with magic was done for visual effect only. I wasn't brave enough to ask why, but Faith didn't have that problem. I overheard her talking at him one day before Lab.

"I don't want us to get behind, is all," she explained. "And I know people in the other class. They're doing real experiments, making solutions with magical precipitates, and infusing materials for use in magicpsychic devices. When will we do that kind of stuff? I'm losing patience."

"Patience or not, science is important, and you will learn every-thing the other class does eventually." The professor sighed. "It's nobody's fault but mine. You see, it was my decision to run an experi-ment that should have commenced during the latter half of the semester, so if you want to blame anybody, blame me."

Faith couldn't argue with that, but she did take it up with Grace, asking her to speak to Professor DeBeer about the experiments in her lab. She flat-out refused, at least the first time, but a couple of weeks later, she came to me and said that Professor DeBeer had moved some of the more complex labs up in the syllabus.

"But why, Grace?"

"She wouldn't tell me. Just dodged around it, sort of." Grace shrugged. "I think she's trying to show Luciano up. She went to all community and state schools, yet still somehow managed to get a tenured position here. That's one reason I think they fight all the time. Luciano went to all the best schools everywhere and had tenure overseas, then came to Hawthorn after getting turned down at Providence Paranormal."

"That's interesting, but not really our business, I guess." I shook my head. "As long as we all end up learning the same stuff and don't have trouble in our second year because of it."

"Do we get new professors next year or what?" Grace rolled her eyes. "It's just that their feud is so annoying. Distracting, too. Where I'm from, when teachers don't get along, they don't fight about it in front of the students."

"I hear you." I nodded. "Maybe it's cultural, but neither of them is from the States, so I don't know what's up. Anyway, we don't get new professors. We're stuck with them for three years."

"Wow. Here's hoping we don't get screwed academically."

The day after that conversation, I found Grace sitting outside the headmaster's office. He invited her in as I walked by, and although I didn't hear their conversation, I was pretty sure it was about the professorial feud. I was glad she'd brought it up. The last thing I wanted was to draw attention to myself while hiding the fact that I was an extramagus. Only the folks right in front had seen me use solar, and if Professor Luciano had said anything, I'd have been summoned to Headmaster Hawkins by now. I still couldn't fathom why he'd stayed mum.

Halfway through September, I started seeing the fliers on the wall. Noah had talked about it before, and it happened at all the specialized schools, so I should've expected it. But it'd be problematic for most of my friends.

I was talking about Parents' Night.

That morning at breakfast, I sat with Hal at our usual booth. A few minutes after I sat down, Dylan and Logan practically bumped into each other, each grasping one of the fliers. They sat down, noticed that they were both upset about the same thing, and began complaining together.

"I don't know what to do, man." Dylan shook his head. "They're just gonna tell me they can't afford to come, and if they do show up, it'll be an endless guiltfest. If they don't come, it'll be Mum writing seventeen letters about how sorry she is they couldn't make it, and how they're bad parents for having no money. If they do show, they'll go gaga over Gale, and draw all sorts of attention to the fact that he doesn't match up with my test scores."

"I wish my parents could just give yours plane tickets and stay home." Logan sighed. "If your folks come on someone else's dime, they can't complain, and I could avoid mom and dad finding out what's been going on around here. You know."

"I've had an idea about that, actually." Hal scribbled a few last-minute sentences on his homework. "Why don't you just swap familiars for the night and pretend things went the other way around?"

"You know, that might actually work." Logan leaned his cheek on one hand. "We're roommates and everything, and my folks know we hang out together, so if we just tell Doris and Gale it's a game, maybe my parental units will chill. It's just for one day."

"My parents wouldn't know how to chill if they got locked in a walk-in freezer." Dylan snorted. "It's probably for the best if mine don't show. But yeah, we can do a switcheroo if it'll make things easier on you, Logan."

"What about Elanor?" I jerked my chin at her table, where she sat with her back to us. "Won't she rat you out?"

"No." Logan shook his head. "Everything's all about her when it comes to Mom and Dad. It's like having a walking photobomb for a sister. She jumps in and does her thing loudly between our parents and me. She won't go out of her way to get me in trouble because it takes attention away from her. That's how it's always been."

"Wow, that sucks." Dylan elbowed Hal good-naturedly in the ribs. "Kinda makes you relieved to be an only child, huh?"

"Maybe." Hal bent his head over his paper, putting the finishing touches on his answer. "But anyway, if this works out, I'll be glad for you guys."

Setting up the critter swap was only the beginning. It ended up taking loads of extra work for Dylan and Logan. So, of course, I made it a point to help. I pulled Grace in on it, too.

Faith tagged along. I wasn't sure why, unless Hal put her up to it somehow. Mostly all she did was hang around and watch. On occasion, Seth and Ember teamed up to try to curb Gale's ego, and maybe that was the answer. Seth wanted to help, and Faith was indulging him. The bonds between familiars and their magi work both ways, after all, and Seth was probably the friendliest Sha in the known universe.

Faith's help turned out to be serendipitous since she got the bright idea to ask Nurse Smith if we could switch familiars as part of our Familiar Studies exercises. That was perfectly valid, but not an activity Nurse Smith or Professor DeBeer had planned for our remedial course, which was about to end. Familiar Studies only went for the first month of school.

In a way, I'd miss going to the extra class. It only felt like a burden when we got a lot of homework assignments. However, having extra time to practice Bishop's Row from October onward would be nice. Our team was coming along well. Okay, that was an understatement.

We'd competed against the other class during the last week of September. I got a chance to see how my friends had managed in their version of Gym with Coach Chen, and we'd won the first game.

Chen wasn't remotely like Pickman. He was not a taskmaster, but his teaching style was effective for some of the students in the other section. Dylan was an absolute terror on the court, someone even I had to watch out for. I had a hard time keeping up with him, and the only player on our team who ever got the jump on him was Hal. The reason we won that game was because his unexpected distraction allowed me to take one last player out along with me. Space magic was super useful in Bishop's Row. Who knew?

The second game had ended in a stalemate, but our times and outs were up there with the second-year teams. Because of that, they decided to include us in Intramurals in spring, a Bishop's Row tournament that was usually for second and third years only.

I guess we all performed well enough for them to add another bracket. That meant we'd make a single team, with tryouts the week before Thanksgiving. Also, I might have to face my brother on the court, which was nerve-wracking, but it was something to worry about later.

The thing on everyone's mind that last week of September was Parents' Night. It'd be a big deal for everyone, and possibly trauma-inducing for half my friends. Of course, they freaked out. Parents' Night wasn't just some tour around campus for the adults; it was also a full social function for us students, including a semi-formal dance.

I had gone stag to all the dances at my old school with Izzy and Cadence, so that didn't bother me, but I worried for my friends, and that made it harder to hide my solar magic. The last thing I wanted was to glow like a firefly in front of everyone. The worst-case scenario was full-on panic with a crowd clamoring for my expulsion. At best, parents would take their kids home, leaving Hawthorn Academy at a low enough attendance to justify closing the school.

Nobody knows for now. Keep it that way.

The only other person who might have noticed was Coach Pickman. In the middle of a game, it was hard to tell whether I combined solar and fire energy, but since she hadn't demanded I flash sunlight in my opponent's eyes, I assumed the inside voice was right.

Still, avoiding detection and worrying about passing as a plain old fire magus was both anxiety-inducing and distracting to such a degree that I neglected an awful lot of items on my to-do list. That was why it wasn't until Thursday, the day before Parents' Night, when I realized something was bothering Grace.

"Are you sure you're going to wear that? To the dance, I mean?"

"I know there's a whole lot of fancy clothes in my closet, Grace, but Noah packed them. Honestly, I prefer just dressing like it's a normal day. You can't trip over skirts if you're not wearing them, right?"

"Well, it's just that, I mean, your parents are coming here to see you look all grown up and stuff. Isn't that a special occasion or something? Or do your parents really not care what you wear?"

"Huh?" The way she'd phrased the questions had me on edge. Not because of her, but for her.

"I know, I know, it's none of my business." She had her back to me, but the hitches in her voice showed despite her efforts to hide them.

"Just, my aunt, well, she can't afford the trek out here." She waved a hand at her ubiquitous jeans and flannel. "Or anything but this for my wardrobe."

"Grace?" My brain couldn't come up with any way to solve her problem, which was similar to Dylan's but worse. She'd only ever mentioned her aunt, wondering aloud about things parents might care about, like she was being hypothetical. My brain finally made the leap.

Grace had no parents, and she didn't want to talk about it, or she wouldn't have hidden it. Nothing I could have offered would help. The only thing in my head was a story told at my bedside in early childhood. One about another orphaned girl and a dance she had no means to attend. I wasn't a changeling and nobody's godmother, but maybe there *was* some small comfort to offer my friend.

"Do you want to borrow something from my closet?"

She turned, eyes wide as she stared at me. Her mouth opened, and her color got high. Had my question embarrassed her?

"I think I'm just going to stay in this room on Parents' Night."

"Why?"

"I just shouldn't go. Nobody will care whether I'm there anyway, even though I like dancing."

"I'd care. I'd miss you if you stayed in here." I watched her shoulders. The trembling in them had slowed. "Besides, Dylan's parents probably won't be there either. I bet he'd love some company."

The moment the words came out of my mouth, I realized I didn't want Grace to go to Parents' Night with Dylan like some sort of date. Because that was what I wanted to do. Ember landed on my shoulder, rubbing cheeks with me. But I had Mom and Dad. Grace and Dylan were in the same boat, alone in a foreign country. Leaning on each other to get through this could help them. What I wanted was less important than what two close friends needed.

"I guess I could ask him." She looked away. "If he says yes, is your offer still good for borrowing something?"

"Yeah, Grace. Always."

She nodded, then grabbed her pajamas and bathroom bag and

headed into the hall. She returned maybe an hour later, much longer than her showers usually took. Her face practically glowed, and her smile was wide as she walked through the door.

"He said, yes!"

We spent the rest of our time before lights out trying things on. It was more fun to pick outfits for a party together than alone.

CHAPTER THIRTEEN

It was the first Saturday I didn't spend at Hawthorne Street. In a way, home came to me because even Bubbe would be here tonight. I was relieved about but extra worried about controlling myself. If she found out what I really was, my relationship with my grandmother might never be the same.

I couldn't talk about it to Grace or Dylan. The two of them had their own problems. I'd have talked to Hal, but he was totally preoccupied with Faith. She was in a near-panicked state, which I should have expected. Seth was so nervous that even Ember's crooning couldn't relax him. If her parents were even remotely like her sister, it was no wonder. I even found myself fearing their arrival.

The only other person I trusted enough was Logan, so I followed him into the library after breakfast. He'd taken to doing all of his class reading in there. It was the most distraction-free place on campus besides the dorm, and at the library, the Ashfords were there to help with questions.

Doris blinked as I strode over. Her surprise must have carried because Logan sat up straight, posture tense. When he recognized me, my friend nodded and waved me over.

"Hey, Aliyah." He was stiff and formal, and I didn't know why.

"What's up?"

"I should be asking you." He cleared his throat. "About what's up, I mean. Besides us this morning. And Ember on the chandelier." A nervous little laugh erupted from his throat.

"Oh, right." I nodded. "Hey, I just came over to ask if we could chat, but now I've got to ask, are you okay?"

"Um, maybe." He folded his hands together, placing them on top of the notepad sitting beside his textbook. His thumbnails were such a wreck I wanted to put antiseptic and bandages on them.

"How can I help?"

"Well, gimme a sec." He took a deep breath. "Will you go to the dance with me?"

"Wait, what?" I stepped back so unconsciously, I tripped over the chair rooted to the floor behind me—and ended up on my backside, of course.

"Oh, no!" Logan jumped out of his seat in a flash, leaning down to give me a hand up.

I took it. When our hands touched, I felt a flash of heat, but no flames appeared. My solar magic acted up, and only the bright light in the library stopped anyone from noticing. If this was my response to a surprise in this comforting environment, I barely stood a chance of escaping detection tonight.

"Thanks, Logan." I got up, a feat made much easier with his help.

He didn't reply, just stood as still as a pond, waiting. Of course, because he'd asked me a question and I'd replied by falling over.

"Yes, I'll go with you." I nodded, grinning. It was a relief, knowing one of my friends would be by my side for most of the evening.

"You mean it?" He got the floor to release the chair, then held it out for me.

"Absolutely." I sat, and he helped me push it in.

"Thank goodness." He settled back into his own seat, posture relaxing. "So, you wanted to chat? It's important, right?"

"Yeah." I told him my problem, how I'd have to work extra hard at hiding my magic. Asked if he had any idea how to go about that.

It wasn't easy. I was ashamed about lying to my parents. My biggest fear was that Logan would judge me.

He totally surprised me.

"You came to the right guy." He nodded. "I mean, my family's all about how to make magic look certain ways. They raised Elanor and me to make it seem larger than life, but reversing some of what they taught me will work."

"We don't have much time. They get in for the assembly before dinner."

"Oh, I know, but don't worry." He grinned. "We're lucky. Most of it is stuff I can do with my water magic. Watch this."

Logan showed me a few tricks around the solar light fixtures. After watching him for less than a minute, I suspected this might work out after all. As long as I could stick with Logan Pierce for the entire event, maybe we'd make it through unscathed.

The four of us waited upstairs until the last minute. None of us really wanted to go down to where the rest of the school happily greeted their families. For a few minutes, I almost thought we'd stay there, in some sort of social limbo between bailing and attending. Then Hal showed up wearing a three-piece suit in jet with a silver vest.

Faith Fairbanks was on his arm, and I mean on. As in, she was dressed to the nines in a black cocktail dress with silver accents. I'd seen runway models while Noah watched Fashion Week who couldn't have held a candle to her.

Seth trotted behind them, his behavior befitting an AKC champion. He glanced at Ember, who dropped the Sha a wink as though she understood it wasn't playtime.

As Hal began escorting Faith down the stairs, walking instead of activating the magical conveyance, he beckoned to the rest of us. Even with his encouragement, we still stood immobile. The real catalyst was his date.

"I refuse to go out there without an entourage." Faith tossed her head, hair cascading over one bare shoulder in chestnut waves. "So, move your butts already."

"Come on, then." Dylan offered his elbow to Grace. "Let's not awaken her inner mean-girl."

"Oh, yeah, don't want that." Grace stepped up beside her date.

"How about it, Logan?" It was up to me to get us moving.

He'd been silent the whole time, except he had one hand clenching hard enough to break the skin on his palms. I recognized that from class, when he made huge efforts to focus and get everything right.

"Are you sure?" He shook his head. "What if it's not perfect? Because I mess things up?"

"We don't have to be perfect, Logan, just present. We can do this."

"Okay." He took a deep breath.

And just like that, we made an entrance so cinematic, our classmates literally talked about it for years. Gale and Doris even managed to remember it was "opposite day," too.

Hal and Faith brought all the glitz, but Dylan and Grace were just as head-turning. I decided to let her keep the purple dress she'd borrowed. The plum flattered her complexion, and the hemline that was too short on me was a perfectly classy knee-length for her stature. Not to mention, the dress's hue represented umbral magic. It was perfect on her, and complimentary to the ice-blue tie Dylan wore.

I noticed my mother watching our descent. Her hand went to her breastbone, and she gazed at me like I'd stepped out of an old photograph. She had good reason. That mint green dress Noah had tossed into my suitcase a month ago had originally belonged to Mom. She'd worn it at this very school on her own Parents' Night years ago. She'd told me this when she hung it in my closet last spring, which Noah encouraged because that style had come back in again this year.

She and Dad must have been on a trip down memory lane, but not Bubbe. Her gaze appraised, as though she analyzed the lot of us and how we had paired off for this event—like she was aware we had a strategy, although she couldn't suspect why when it came to anyone besides the boys.

Logan's parents also studied us. Their eyes narrowed at first until they caught themselves making unflattering faces. After that, they both put on figurative masks, but in that short span of time, I understood their confusion. They expected to see us together but perhaps not clinging so tightly. I mean, we were, but not in an inappropriate way.

The worst were the Fairbanks. They took one look at the lot of us on the stairs and turned their backs like they didn't even care that their middle daughter was dating the headmaster's son.

Yeah, they actually were dating. Hal looked practically giddy, and while Faith's face wore its usual expression of deliberate ennui, she went farther than just putting one hand on his arm. Instead, their hands were twined together like a litter of sleepy Sha pups. There was a comfort and solidarity in that gesture, one I'd seen before.

Between my parents.

The mean girl and the nice guy. Who knew?

At the bottom of the stairs, it was easy enough to navigate to our seats for the assembly. We took up an entire row, so no worries about sitting next to any enemies. Kitty's group went in behind us like they were playing rear guard, or maybe they were also avoiding Charity and her minions. Not that they could get up to much with this many parents plus all the faculty and staff in attendance. Even Zeke was there, standing in the back with Penelope.

Our parents sat on the other side of the aisle. Seats were marked out for them, so the ones who hadn't been here before weren't confused. I counted heads and looked for familiar faces. As we expected, Dylan's folks hadn't come.

Headmaster Hawkins appeared literally out of nowhere, silencing the din of cross-chatter. He clapped his large hands until the chatter died down, then cleared his throat to begin his speech.

"Welcome, families! Some of you for the first time, and others for the second or third. Tonight, you will tour the campus and see some of the projects our students have been working on. After a divine dinner prepared by our newest chef, we'll have a mixer with dancing. I'm an educator, not a public speaker, so I'll keep this brief. Thank you, students. Without your dedicated and excellent work, we'd have nothing to show your families this evening. Now, go and enjoy the evening together!"

He clapped his hands once again, not in dismissal of the crowd, but for himself. The headmaster vanished immediately after, while the echo still lingered at the corners of the room. More than a few parental-aged women, here without a date, sighed in dismay.

There was something to Cadence's gossip columns after all.

The group of us stuck together during the tour. Logan's parents chattered away at my folks but didn't say a word to Bubbe. Logan leaned in, whispering that this was typical for them. They didn't bother with anyone my grandmother's age. Their loss.

The Fairbanks took a moment to say hello to the Pierces as we sauntered through the academic hallway, but they totally ignored Faith. Her mom, who looked almost exactly like Charity, gave me one withering glare, and that was it. They ignored my parents.

The entire time we were on the tour, Gale stayed perched obediently on Logan's shoulder. It helped that Ember peeped at him the whole time. He chirped back, too, which made me wonder what they were talking about.

Because Logan and I brought up the rear, we noticed that Lune and Doris had a modified game of tag going. Each time the mercat reached out with a paw, the moon hare hopped out of the way. On occasion, it was Lune moving sideways toward Doris, who dodged just in time.

I hadn't seen Nin and Seth in a while, so I looked around for them. They were in the last place I expected—in Faith's tote, cuddling, which would have been cute if familiars usually got that friendly with each other. I'd seen it exactly once before, in the one photo Bubbe keeps of her parents on their wedding day.

Were my friends in love?

I spent the rest of the tour studying them, looking for clues, but either Faith and Hal were both better actors than Logan's slick entertainment family or were still unaware of their potential.

The idea that something positive could come from our defensive social maneuvers had me walking on air. That was why I spent most of the dinner hour smiling at everyone, even Noah when he sat with Elanor at our table. This was the first time in a month he'd even looked at me. He rolled his eyes immediately and started whispering in his bestie's ear, but even that couldn't get me down.

After dinner, we almost had a collective heart attack. All of the familiars went to their corner for their meal, as usual. But when they returned, Gale and Doris forgot about opposite day.

Logan froze. Doris leaping up into his lap wasn't at all what he expected. My date couldn't roll with those punches, so I did.

"Aww, look!" I pointed at the mercat, doing my best impression of Cadence. "Dylan and Logan are such good friends, they even get along with each other's familiars. So cute!"

Ember played along, stopping on the back of Grace's chair to ruffle her hair before returning to me. She peeped at Gale for good measure, who got the message and only chirped at Dylan before landing on Logan's shoulder.

Doris put her paws on Logan's chest, stretching up to rub cheeks with Gale. Once they made their greeting, she jumped off Logan's lap and padded back to Dylan, who scooped her up for a cuddle and a scratch behind the ears.

Once dinner was over, we headed back out of the cafeteria and into the lobby. Streamers hung from the walls, and the solar lights flashed and pulsed under globes of various spell effects. From the looks of concentration on faculty faces, they'd worked hard to make the occasion literally magical. Earthbound familiars scooted to the sides, while winged ones made way for their magi by fluttering toward perches or the rafters.

Logan stepped lightly across the space between the seats at the sidelines and the dance floor. He must have been looking forward to this all night because we were the first ones there, arriving a breath before the music started—a waltz, but popular. *With a Little Help from My Friends*, the Joe Cocker version. His easy smile meant he was in his element here.

"I can't dance," I managed.

"That's okay, nobody will know." He leaned closer, voice low beside my ear. "Even if you get nervous, they won't see anything they shouldn't."

"How?" My hands were already warmer.

"Pretend I'm a mirror and copy me." He put one of my hands on his shoulder and held the other, pressing our palms together.

Our arms made a frame. I clung to that, and he was right. The soft glow of his water magic hid everything. When solar light gleamed between our hands, he narrowed his eyes and magical focus until it flickered like my good old flames instead.

My tension eased, loosening its grip until I could forget about being an extramagus. Almost.

As we moved together, traveling across the dance floor, a series of startled gasps followed us. When we passed our friends, clapping and low whistles took over. If Hal and Faith had made the biggest entrance, we made up for it now with sheer entertainment value.

For once, my legs didn't feel coltish and clumsy, and being at eye level with my dance partner made all the difference in my ability to focus and do more than let him lead. We circled past our siblings and parents. Logan's mother was still stone-faced, but his dad's lips wore a small smile. Noah stood, slack-jawed and wide-eyed, only snapping out of it when Elanor elbowed him in the ribs and dragged him off to dance too. My father had his arm around my mom. They swayed together, grinning.

Bubbe studied us like critters under her care, which made sense because she knew more than Mom or Dad about the trouble Logan and I had at school. She didn't take this at face value like everybody else in the room because she knew better. She paid more attention to Logan than me, though.

I made it through the entire song, but even better, we danced to three more before I was out of breath. We regrouped at a table with a cascading fountain of punch. I didn't dare leave Logan's side, even though it sort of ruined the attempted chivalry in his act of fetching me a drink. Judging by his smile, he either didn't mind or understood.

Dylan and Grace trotted over, huffing and puffing after their turn around the dance floor. They didn't do anything nearly as structured or formal as waltzing, though.

"How 'bout that chicken dance, hey?" Grace chuckled.

"More fun than a barrel of monkeys." Dylan smirked. "But we're talentless hacks, of course."

"Here's to Team Hack!" Logan raised his glass.

Faith sauntered out of the shadows, Hal in tow. She was still cool as a cucumber, but he shuffled his feet with a furrowed brow. Just as I wondered what the two of them were up to, hiding out together in the corner, she told me.

"Watch your back, Aliyah." Faith reached out, putting a hand on my shoulder. "Charity's going to try something."

"Why?"

"She's jealous, of course. Does she need another reason?"

"But I didn't do anything."

"You don't have to." She shook her head. "I'm going to try to deflect her, but this is your warning. Avoid the twins, okay?"

"Thanks, Faith."

"Don't thank me. Just do as I say."

I nodded. Logan stood beside me as Faith stalked off. Hal followed her at a distance like a satellite. They circled the dance floor like gulls over the beach at low tide.

As the last song ended, Charity detached from her dance partner and strolled toward us, eyes on the punch bowl.

"Let's make like eggs and beat it," said Grace.

The lot of us hustled away from the refreshment table, heading toward some of the seats at the other end of this side of the dance floor. On the way, we passed the twins. One of them stuck a foot out, trying to trip me. I got tangled and almost toppled over despite my sensibly flat shoes.

Logan grabbed me around the waist, literally sweeping me off my feet. At his touch, I was buoyant, as though immersed in water. He spun us in a circle in the direction of the dance floor, and then we were out there, stopping the show again.

As we navigated around the other couples, which included my parents, I noticed Faith and Charity facing off beside the punch bowl. My friend trembled until Hal stepped behind her, placing his hand on the table. As the sisters argued, I watched Charity grasp the tablecloth and pull, toppling the entire fountain toward Faith.

It vanished for a moment, during which Hal pulled Faith into a hug. When the fruit-punch fountain reappeared, it was directly over Charity's head, spilling its contents all over her. Faith and Hal faded into the shadows. I spotted Grace in the corner, eyes narrowed, with one finger directed at their vanishing point.

Charity Fairbanks stood with the tablecloth in her hand, soaked from head to toe in fruit punch. It looked like she'd had an embarrassing accident.

The room went silent, the lights low-watt incandescent. My hands felt like blacktop in the middle of July. Everyone's focus sat squarely on Queen Mean, but once my hands lit up, it'd be all over for me.

"Oh, shit."

"Shh, I've got you."

And Logan did. He led me to the bottom stair, then named our floor to start it moving. As it rose, light poured from my hands, and my date had that covered too. Literally.

Globes of water surrounded the fists I made, turning the solar flares inside them into what looked like fire underwater. It was dim enough for me to escape with Logan up the stairs. A few heads turned, one of them Professor Luciano's. Our teacher was the only one who didn't mistake it for a deliberate farewell display.

At the top of the stairs, we almost tripped over Hal and Faith. They were on the floor, leaning against the wall together. Both smiled, although Hal looked pretty beat.

"Let's get out of here."

"That's the only time you've talked sense, Pierce." Faith snorted. "Come on." She didn't exactly help Hal up as much as scoop him off the floor, but the end result was the same.

We all headed down the hall, where Faith helped an unsteady and exhausted Hal negotiate the route to his room. Logan paused.

"I've got to say goodnight to my parents." He almost ran right into our roommates.

"They're already gone." Dylan shook his head. "Sorry, man." Gale swooped down and landed on his shoulder.

"That's okay." Doris trotted up and rubbed against Logan's legs. He reached down to scratch her ears. "All in all, I think we did all right."

"Yeah." I held out my arm to give Ember a place to land.

"Did you see Charity's face?" Grace leaned against the wall, holding her sides. Lune was beside her, kicking his feet up. "She looked like a B-movie vampire from back before the Reveal!"

We all had a laugh at that because the last thing Charity Fairbanks would ever want was to look remotely like a vampire. It felt like fitting payback for all the abuse she'd dished out to the undead staff and her own sister.

The boys walked Grace and me to our room. I thanked them both and opened the door, stopping so Logan and I could wave to each other. Dylan lingered, Grace remaining outside with him.

When she came back in, her face was even more flushed than when she'd laughed. Her lip gloss was smudged, too. That meant my roommate and her crush had hit it off, on top of all the other stuff we'd managed with our hard work and preparation. Something different had happened with Logan and me. We understood each other, anyway, and I could trust him.

If this were an exam, we would have passed with flying colors. My ultimate goal was hiding what I really was. I'd met that and then some. Our entire group might have just leveled up socially, too.

So why did I feel sad?

CHAPTER FOURTEEN

It was midweek, and I went home right after Lab. No, I didn't get expelled. It was *Erev Yom Kippur*, the eve of Yom Kippur and the most important holiday my family observed. Hawthorn Academy had always let students keep their individual faiths, which was why I was walking down Essex Street a half-hour before sunset with Noah, who still wasn't talking to me.

The biggest indirect lesson I'd learned at Hawthorn Academy: doing good was Punk AF.

I'd secretly hoped my brother and I would settle things after the punchbowl incident. That somehow, he'd see how ridiculous it was, marching to the beat of an unusually cruel bigot's drum. I even wore his discarded Vamp Lives Matter shirt that day, but it was no use. He wasn't interested in joining my kindness rebellion.

That was what I'd been doing all week since Parents' Night—my friends too—going out of our way to thank the vampires on staff in front of other people. Making it a point to hold doors, even for people we didn't like. Helping folks when they dropped something. Inviting the rest of our year to study groups.

And it was catching on, slowly but noticeably. Even Hailey stopped snickering when Logan got called on and stuttered an answer. I caught Coach Pickman helping Coach Chen with Bishop's Row trunks. And Noah's ex, Darren, had more of his classmates at his study group, kids who weren't doing so well academically.

The biggest change was in Faith. She smiled more, laughed longer, and with people more often than at them. That was more likely because of Hal, though. They lit each other up, reminding me for all the world of Mom and Dad. At first, I thought they made me homesick, but that wasn't right. Maybe during my break, I'd figure it out. Yom Kippur was the day to reflect on the previous year, after all.

I glanced at Noah as we approached the corner of Hawthorne Street. He looked away, down at the wheeled suitcase he'd overpacked instead of meeting my gaze. I adjusted my knapsack and waited through his luggage hiccup before walking along. His attitude didn't justify me leaving him behind, no matter how satisfying it might have been to walk away and leave him in distress. He was my brother, and I'd help him if he needed it.

Doing the right thing was harder than giving up, but that was how I knew this was the right track. Well, one way. Lotan peeked out from under Noah's collar, bobbing his head at me. The serpent appreciated my gesture, at least.

My brother tossed away the stone jamming his suitcase's wheel, then continued on. We walked past Izzy's house and down the driveway toward 10-1/2, and just like that, we were home.

Lunch wasn't that long ago. All the same, Bubbe had set out a loaf of challah bread in a braided circle as she always makes it for Yom Kippur. Sliced apples, honey, and dried apricots accompanied it, with iced lemon tea to wash it down. Noah and I sat in silence at the counter, having the last food we'd eat over the next twenty-four hours. After that, I washed my face and wrapped a white pashmina shawl around my shoulders to get ready for the services. Ember burrowed under it, draping herself across my shoulders in the process.

Dad and Bubbe each lit a yahrzeit, the memorial candle, for Grandpa and Bubbe's parents. Five minutes later, we headed to our temple across the bridge in Beverly.

The synagogue was full, like it had been every year for as long as I can remember. We were secular Jews, not Orthodox or even Conservative. Surely, you've heard of Easter-and-Christmas Christians? Well, we were the Jewish equivalent, but it wouldn't have felt like the High Holy Days if we weren't there. Bubbe reminded us that the freedom we had to celebrate publicly was a privilege our ancestors didn't always have.

I refused to take it for granted, not after I was old enough to hear the stories about our great-grandpa's escape from Poland.

We took seats together. Don't be surprised by this. Our synagogue was egalitarian, which meant men and women sat together instead of in different sections. Noah sat so our parents were between us, but this had happened in previous years inadvertently, so they didn't think it was strange.

I knew better.

As Cantor David sang the Kol Nidre prayer, we listened. It was all about how we came to temple on the holiest day of our year to be absolved of obligations, bonds, and other pressures put upon us under duress. Historically, this came from ages past, when Jews living in those times were forced to convert or die. The Spanish Inquisition was a prime example, though certainly not the first.

We were freed from burdens like this by singing this prayer.

This year, the words had a striking impact. Renouncing vows made under duress meant giving up Ember. We'd bonded after a moment of extreme agony for her and stress for me, after all, but I also realized that release was important exactly because of this.

So I focused my thoughts on her, making it clear that she was free to go if I wasn't the right magus for her.

At that moment, with my familiar's tail curled around my arm, I was acutely aware that she'd agreed to renew our bond, without the baggage this time, and that reinforced its strength.

My mind took me back to a sunlit day more than a decade ago, before my grandfather passed. Ember made the trip back through my memory by my side.

"Scars are tougher than unblemished skin." Grandpa finished wrapping the gauze over the sterile pad.

"But it hurts." I sniffled, but it was no use. The trickle under my nose wouldn't budge.

"It's got to hurt if it's to heal." My grandfather tore paper tape. "And once it does, that sidewalk will have a devil of a time trying to skin that knee again."

"Really, Grampy?" I blinked, tears drying sticky on my cheeks.

"And how." His eyes twinkled.

Before I remembered my response, the present dragged back me back again.

My mouth moved, reciting three times the prayers of forgiveness I knew by heart.

When the services were over, we headed home. Usually, we'd be quiet and contemplative like this each year. We all had tons to reflect on, although that was the first time I was fully aware of how hard it must have been for Mom. She never once complained about not getting to see her relatives.

Clearly, her brother Richard was a seriously bad egg, but what about her parents? She must have missed them, even if she was estranged from them, like Dylan missed his. Maybe she felt more like Grace—a stranger to typical family dynamics.

This time of year, we did an awful lot of reflecting, especially when it came to stuff like my horrible extramagus secret. I was torn because the right thing to do wasn't clear here. If my life were a video game, both of my choices were Nightmare Mode.

Don't tell Mom my secret. She was still stuck without half her family, wondering whether they were well or even alive, except for Richard, whose fate was being decided on national news. And she got to wonder whether either of her children would grow up to be like her brother.

Tell Mom my secret. She'd still be stuck like now, but in that scenario, she'd know it was me she had to worry about. I'd turn evil someday and end up in prison or worse.

Both of those sucked.

"What was that, Bissel?" Bubbe sat in the middle of the back seat between Noah and me.

"Just my inside voice escaping again." I sighed.

"Well, at least this is the day for it." She reached out, taking my hand.

"I'll do all that when we get home."

But it took longer than that. Hours, in fact.

Later that night, despite being ready for bed, I couldn't sleep. So I got up, leaving Ember asleep at the foot of the bed. Last year I would have paced my room, but that was impossible now unless I wanted to give myself a concussion and spend the rest of the holiday at Salem Hospital, so I headed downstairs.

The television was on, so I walked into the living room where Mom sat up alone. She wasn't really looking at the screen, just staring out the window, so I took a seat beside her and tucked my feet up under my legs.

"I hope you're getting enough sleep at school," she said.

"Yeah. The day usually wipes me out."

There was a pause, not just between us but from the TV, too. We both decided that was a good time to talk.

"I'm sorry—"

"Mom, I—"

I blinked, but she chuckled.

"Who should go first?" she asked.

"You, I guess, Mom."

"Aliyah, I'm sorry." She sighed. "I should have mentioned Richard sooner. Well, maybe not just him, but also where I came from. The family who raised me and why I left them behind when I made my own family here. Half of you is me, and half of me is them. Raising you and Noah halfway like that wasn't the right thing to do."

"Why, then?"

"I thought it would protect you. Not physically, but your hearts. I saw how afraid of everything your brother was, and how you have such a hard time loving yourself, and I didn't want to make it worse. You're both so strong when you forget all that and just act, and now I bet nobody on that campus is letting you forget that you're both Hopewells."

The silence struck like a Tallin Serpent guarding a nest. It hadn't hit me until just now that Noah got his own share of grief over Richard, even though I was the one who resembled him. Maybe he wasn't ignoring me because he hated me now. Maybe he was scared, even if I'd never thought of my big brother that way before.

Older siblings had a sort of armor. Izzy's one, plus she has one, and she'd told me this before. The younger kids think the older ones are like Superman, impervious to almost everything, and with extra abilities to boot.

After all this time, it turned out he wasn't. I should have listened to my best friend. I'd have to go apologize to her tomorrow...but I'd left my mother hanging.

"Mom, I forgive you." I opened my arms, and the hug she gave me was warm and welcoming if a little tear-stained. "I love you."

"I love you, too." After we let go, she pulled a tissue from her sleeve and dabbed her eyes. "Okay. It's your turn, Aliyah."

I still didn't know what to say. The choices in front of me were the Lady and the Tiger, but for me, there was a door number three.

"I made a ton of assumptions about all this for the whole month." I waved my hand at nothing, but her face told me she understood. "The why and the how about the Hopewells, and I know you must have worried all that time. Wondering whether I was mad, whether I was really busy every weekend or just avoiding you. But Mom, I'm sorry. I did avoid talking to you about it, how some of the kids at school pick on me because of my uncle. And I'm sorry."

"I forgive you. But you've talked to someone about it? It's important to take care of your health in all ways."

"Yeah, I talked to my friends. And Bubbe, a little."

"Aliyah, I'm proud of you."

I sat back, not daring to speak. Right now, all the words wanted to come out—the ones I shouldn't say until I was sure she was ready to hear them. The truth.

All my focus was on keeping my hands from glowing, and it was a miracle because it worked.

We thanked each other and then Mom said goodnight, heading upstairs to bed.

It was empty down there, so I sat for a while, not really looking at the *Buffy* reruns Mom had been watching. I thought I was all alone because Bubbe couldn't possibly have been down in her office at this time of night, so I scooted over, cozying up to the box of tissues and just let the tears come.

It was a knock-down-drag-out ugly cry.

That was what I got for holding back tears for a month and change. A deluge. A flood. The microbes living on my face should have gotten into an ark, two by two. Biblical floods of tears felt extra, even on this high holy day.

"Bissel?"

It was Bubbe. Of course, she was downstairs in her office instead of up in her bedroom. She crossed the living room like a ship on storm-tossed waters pulling into the shore. Her hand rubbed my back, a comfort sorely missed.

"Oh, Bubbe. I'm so tired of it all."

She said nothing, just pulled me into a hug. It never mattered to my grandmother why or how I got in a state like this. She just didn't want me going through it alone. She treated my brother the same way, which was why her next words didn't surprise me.

"Noah's tired of it too." She kept rubbing my back. "That was why I told him to talk to you already."

"You noticed?" I pulled back to see her face.

"That you two weren't speaking? Yes. And he wants to apologize if you give him the chance, although he knows that's not guaranteed."

"I'll listen, Bubbe."

"Good. I'll have water for the two of you downstairs tomorrow morning. Seven-thirty." She studied my face. "Now, go have a wash and get some sleep. You need rest while fasting, after all."

"So do you." I made use of some tissues. "But you were down there all this time, helping the animals."

"Right, because it's our responsibility to care for them. And each other. Remember, a meaningful life is within our reach, if only we—"

"Choose to care," I finished the sentence with her. It wasn't just a thing she said, but a core belief we have as faithful Jews, even if we were pretty secular. Trying to make the world better by caring was our duty.

We hugged once more before saying goodnight. As I headed upstairs, my steps were lighter.

Maybe I wasn't as far off course as I thought.

At the table downstairs, we sat together over water. Bubbe bustled in the hall nearby, feeding and watering the handful of critters in her care. For once, Noah, the king of extra, kept it simple.

"Truce?" he asked.

"I want to be your friend again, Noah. I can't stop caring."

"We can't act friendly at school." He sighed. "Not beyond nods and waves. Too dangerous. You've seen what Charity does to her enemies, and if she thinks I switched sides, she'll torment us both worse than she does to you now."

"Yeah, I know. And you gave danger a hard pass before I was born."

"Mood. Anyway, do you accept?"

"For now, but I'm going to try repairing our relationship as well if it's all the same to you."

"Whatever. But I can't afford to play in your little Mean People Suck sandbox, Aliyah."

"I understand. But who knows? Maybe things will change, and so will your mind. At any rate, I didn't mean to scare you. Fire bad, girl sorry."

"And I'm sorry for pretending you don't exist."

"See? That wasn't so hard."

"Peep."

"Ssss."

"Two out of two familiars agree." I dropped him a wink. The grin he gave back was barely there, but I'd take it.

Back at temple that afternoon, we attended more services. After last night, I felt like I should stay for Yizkor, the memorial part of Yom

Kippur services. Noah and I used to stay out with the other kids our age and younger. There was a superstition that attending while your parents were alive was inviting trouble, but I wanted to remember my grandfather. There had to be a reason he had come so strongly to mind during the opening service yesterday, and honoring that felt right.

The Cantor sang some prayers and the Rabbi read, but the heft of the service came during silent prayer, read to ourselves from books. Standing, we recited Ancestor of Mercies, and Yizkor was almost over. Just one part remained.

Tzedakah, which is an act of charity. I must have somehow known I'd do this part of the service, because I actually had a few dollars to put in the box.

After that, the final sprint toward the end of the holiday began. Neilah, the closing of the gates. Noah and the other young folks came back in as the ending started. This was our last chance to atone for the previous year.

The ark, where the Torah scrolls stayed most of the time, was closed as everyone recited.

"*Seal us in the Book of Life.*"

Now we literally had minutes to affirm our faith, praise God's name, and deny idolatry of any over Him. We did it together as a family within the congregation.

When the Rabbi blew the Shofar horn, it was over.

But it was also the beginning of a new year, one in which I'd vowed to do better. And as we left the temple to break our fast at home, I silently prayed that I was up to the challenge.

CHAPTER FIFTEEN

Overall, my prayers were answered. Or maybe I answered them myself. Either way, it wasn't easy. Serious effort was involved, energy spent on hiding my solar magic and keeping my temper at bay. Choosing kindness over retribution didn't come easily for me anyplace but inside my head.

I wasn't doing it alone, and all through the rest of October, I was grateful for my friends and for Ember. The campus would have been a pile of ashes if it weren't for them, so I made it a point to thank them, even for the small stuff.

Halfway through the month, Headmaster Hawkins announced that we'd have an all-day outing into Salem on Halloween. That meant my friends and all the other students got to see and participate in the parades, concerts, and general festive atmosphere I had experienced every year in town.

Everyone was excited, even the teachers. They decorated their classrooms, including the gym and the library. Grace came running into our room one night, saying that Professor DeBeer gave her permission to work in Creatives for extra time to make her costume. Her excitement was almost palpable and I joined her, kicking off over a week of early mornings and late nights spent working with textiles and sewing machines.

Dylan was there too, even though he said his wardrobe idea was easy. Mostly, I thought he liked the excuse to spend extra time with Grace. We also worked on the costumes during Creatives period each day, drawing no small amount of attention from our classmates. Even though Hal and Faith had ordered their outfits, they looked on with us. Alex and his clique checked on our progress at least twice a day.

Sewing was a pretty obscure skill here at good old Hawthorn Academy. I learned loads about it from Grace, who was a master. She could have been a cosplayer, while I walked into it with the basic skill of how to reattach a button. Good thing my idea was relatively simple.

I wasn't sure why I was so excited about wearing another mask. Maybe because the holiday was all about disguise, or because I wouldn't be the only person wearing one for the day. Pick whichever you'd like and run with it, I guess.

Once again, I caught Luciano and DeBeer arguing heatedly, except this time, it wasn't about lab safety or course materials. It was far more festive than that.

"I don't care what you say, *Lucy*. They're talented for sure, but I just can't stand the way they conduct themselves in interviews."

"They've got heart, and one of the most important causes in the post-Reveal world, *Miss Susie*. And don't call me Lucy, it's Luciano. Professor, if you're being horrible."

"Are you sure we're talking about the same band?" She snorted. "And I'll call you what I like. What are you gonna do about it anyway, cry?"

I trotted off, increasing my speed to catch up with Logan. I wasn't sure I wanted to hear more. Disagreements about music were all fine and well, but our teachers were getting too personal, and I didn't want to witness any weird fallout. I was still curious whether there was some deeper reason why they were constantly at odds, though.

In the last four days leading up to Halloween, Penelope put treats in our dinner bags. On Monday, we sat in the lounge, grinning at the jack o' lantern-shaped cookies adorned with orange and black frosting.

"Oh, ho ho, I'm Santa Pumpkin, coming to bring candy corns down your chimney on Halloween Night!" Hal held his cookie in front of his mouth and nose.

"Eeeek!" Faith leaned back with her hands on her cheeks. "No! Anything but the worst candy ever!"

Everybody laughed, even Darren, who had come by to chat for once.

"I hear you have quite the craft project going on," he said.

"Me? No, I'm just making a mask." I jerked my thumb at the corner, where my roommate sat with headphones on, hunched over some stubborn homework. "It's Grace who's doing big things with fabric."

"Well, regardless, we're all waiting to see how it all looks in a few nights." He smiled, waving as he left. "Happy studying!"

On Tuesday, Penelope gave us cups of chocolate pudding with gummy worms inside. I knew from peeking into the cafeteria while passing that these weren't the usual fare, so I decided to ask Dylan what he knew about the special treats.

"Oh, those are from the café." He grinned. "They're test batches, really. The rest of the school won't get to try these until lunchtime on Thursday."

"Wow."

"Do you know there's a rumor that Penelope is dating the new vampire chef?" Faith studied her nails as she perched on the arm of the cushy chair her boyfriend sat in. "Scandalous, they say."

"No." Hal shook his head, but he reached out, and Faith took his hand. "Well, it shouldn't be, not in a perfect world."

"World's flawed. Sucks to be Gaia." Grace shrugged. "But what else is new?"

"Hey, but aren't we trying to do our best here?" Logan waved his hand at the lot of us, but he looked right at me. "Make it even just a little better?"

"Yeah." I nodded. "And this whole campus plus the entire town outside it has an enormous party coming up. More chances to shake all the haters off."

"Please don't tell me you're planning some sort of Taylor Swift flash mob, Aliyah." Faith closed her eyes, leaning against the back of Hal's comfy chair-and-a-half.

"Definitely not." I chuckled, glancing at Logan. "I can't dance that way."

Wednesday, the dessert in the bag was a cupcake. You might guess the decoration because Logan's reaction was to yeet it across the room.

Yup. It looked like a tarantula.

It was inside a clear plastic clamshell case, though, so it was still good. Doris trotted over to retrieve it, the package crackling in her teeth as she carried it back. When she dropped it at Logan's feet, she curled her tail around her haunches and purred.

"Yeah, okay, Doris. You're a good girl, but I still think someone else should pick that up?" Logan shuddered. "I've got a bad case of arachnophobia."

"Here, let me help with that." I took the cupcake from Doris, then opened the package. Using the knife that came with our dinner bags, I cut the legs off the sides and the mandibles off the front. After that, I grabbed a handful of trick-or-treat-sized Twizzlers from my bag, the kind you peel. Once I arranged them on the spider's legless body, the dessert had a completely different look.

"Ta-da!" I held it out for Logan's inspection, but he still had one hand over his eyes. "It's harmless, I promise."

"A ladybug?"

"Uh-huh." I grinned. "Definitely not a spider pretending to be something else."

"Aliyah Morgenstern, I could kiss you."

Our friends went so silent you could have heard a pin drop. As far as I knew, everyone else had gone there except us, but I think for Logan and me, things were different, even though we'd had plenty of perfect moments for that since Parents' Night.

I liked Logan. He might have been frighteningly pretty and somewhat awkward, but he was also sweet and kind. I had no idea what his motives were. Maybe that was the problem.

I wasn't sure if he was serious. It was impossible to tell whether he was into me or not lately. The dynamic that reminded me of Azreal Ambersmith had vanished since the dance. I should be as certain as possible before I said or did anything definitive.

My concerns weren't entirely emotional. They were practical, too. Heightened emotions plus new situations might equal solar magic surprise. Also, Logan's discomfort was plain to see on his face.

"Uh, we gotta talk about this later," I managed.

Conversation picked up again, the usual banter that almost had its own personality in our group. But it was a little too loud and slightly strained, as though it were a clock somebody had wound too tight.

After dinner, we went our separate ways, and Logan didn't follow me. I couldn't blame him, but maybe we'd get a moment the next day. We all got a half-day and left campus after lunch. I knew Salem proper like the back of my hand. If anyone could find a secluded corner, even on the busiest night in town, it was me.

Lunch was more spectacular than we'd imagined. I know we were all used to spellwork as an everyday part of our lives. All the same, the meal made every student at Hawthorn Academy realize we shouldn't take magic for granted.

Sandwiches were cut into shapes and stacked to look like spooky faces gazing up from plates. Stews swirled in bowls, shimmering with effects that made them look like glitter bath bombs. Everything was totally delicious. We didn't stand in line for our food; instead, it got delivered right to our tables by amazing magical animals.

Not all of the kitchen staff had familiars—it wasn't a requirement for working here, after all—but enough of them did to make even the delivery of the food a stunning presentation. Sandy led a line of other four-legged familiars, equipped with trays on their backs.

"The waitstaff is totally amazing!" Grace clapped her hands, eyes wide with wonder.

"I never would have thought of anything like this." I shook my head. "Say what you will about my brother, but at least he's good at keeping spoilers a secret."

The desserts weren't a surprise, which was a good thing for Logan. He escaped the cafeteria with two pudding cups and a quartet of cookies wrapped in a napkin before the spider cupcakes came out. The rest of us made shorter work of our desserts than the rest of the students in our year, which was good since we needed the extra time.

Upstairs, I helped Grace put on the costume she'd worked so hard on, and it was amazing. I felt almost bad that mine was only a mask with a couple of other accessories, but at least we went together.

"Ready?" I stood at the door, waiting to open it.

"Okay." Grace nodded.

Students lined the hall, waiting to see the big costume reveal, and they weren't disappointed. Ember and Lune peeped and stamped their approval as well. Of course, they were elated.

We had dressed as each other's familiars.

My half-mask gave me a pink nose, whiskers, and connected to the ears on top of my head. The rest of my outfit was a soft silvery-gray cardigan over gray leggings. Of course, it was Grace who took the cake.

She was dressed from head to toe in gilt fabric. A set of golden spikes and whiskers sat on the top of her head, connected at the bottom to her own half-mask in the shape of a dragonet's muzzle. On her body was a golden jumpsuit she had sewed, but the main attraction was the set of fully articulated wings stretching between her back and arms.

In the hall, Grace raised her hands, revealing the wings. I bet she could have glided down the staircase on them if she wanted to, but she didn't. Instead, my roommate activated the stairs and headed down like it was any other day.

It was only a short walk through the lobby and out the door, but what a difference a handful of steps made. Outside on Essex Street danced a scene of particolored celebratory chaos. Mundanes and extrahumans alike flooded the streets, and we walked with the current of folks headed toward Salem Commons.

That was the park enclosed by yards of French Gothic picket fencing in the middle of town, complete with walking paths, a playground at one corner, and a bandstand. Vendors had set up tables, carts, and food trucks along the fence. Some of them were from out of town, but most were staffed and stocked by town shops and restaurants.

I led my friends immediately to one of them, where I saw a familiar face.

"Izzy!" My smile was so big it hurt my face.

"Aliyah? Is that you under there?"

"Yeah."

"Holy guacamole!" Izzy pointed at Grace. "That's the most amazing costume I've ever seen, and I've lived in Halloween Central my whole life."

Her opinion was far from unique. Loads of passersby stopped to ask Grace for pictures and ask if she'd entered one of the many costume contests. She hadn't, in part because many of those are in the 21+ bars, but it gave me an idea—one that'd get my roomie some recognition, and possibly a little money, too.

I strode off, leaving my friends at Izzy's booth, where they waited to get card or palm readings from Izzy's parents. I overheard Dylan trying to turn it down due to the cost, but Hal offered to pay for everyone, even Lee, Eston, and Kitty, who showed up as I walked away.

My goal was the bandstand, where the emcee for the evening's festivities stood directing the road crew. I knew him, of course, because it was Michael Ambersmith, Azrael's dad.

"Well, if it isn't young Miss Morgenstern. Novel costume. Moon hare, is it?" He raised one ruddy eyebrow. "Are you entering the town costume contest?"

"No, I'm here to enter my roommate. Grace DuBois." I pointed her out.

"Wow." He stroked his mustache, appraising her work from a distance. "That's something else. She ordered that online?"

"No, she made it herself in Creatives."

"Your roommate has some serious talent, then." He nodded. "Consider her entered. Wait here, and I'll note her down on the list and bring her number back to you."

I leaned against the nearest column instead of sitting on the bandstand's steps like I'd usually do. The last thing I wanted was to get in the way of the roadies as they set things up for this year's musical guests. Because I'd been on campus so much, I hadn't had a chance to find out who was playing, so I glanced at the poster near my head.

"Night Creatures!?" I almost toppled over.

"Yeah." The voice behind me was deep and mirthful but totally unfamiliar. I turned around to see who was talking to me. I recognized him instantly from the news.

"Fred Redford?" I blinked. "From Tinfoil Hat?"

"Sort of." He shrugged. "Just helping some friends."

"Wow!" I tried to recover and maintain some semblance of calm and decorum. "I mean, that's cool."

In case you were wondering why I was so flustered, it was because they were one of my role models. Fred was part of the Tinfoil Hat Pack, the group of students who'd played a major part in putting the extrahuman world back together a few years ago.

More specifically, they'd thwarted Uncle Richard's attempt to subjugate humans and take over both faerie courts, and now he and a bunch of his friends were here in Salem.

I was so glad I had decided to wear a mask.

Fred threw his head back and laughed so hard tears formed at the corners of his eyes. It was the last thing I expected from a Redcap, even a Seelie one. His laughter attracted the attention of another hero, a woman with long dark hair who set a violin down in a case before sauntering over. It was Irina Kazynski, also famous for being an awesome musician.

"What's so funny, Lunk?" She elbowed him in the ribs, smirking.

"It's just, we've got a fan." His smile could have cut diamonds. "Which rocks."

"What else is new?"

"Not you. We. Plural. As in, Tinfoil Hat."

"Really?" she asked me.

"Yeah." My giggle came out with a snort at the end, like Izzy's. "I mean, you all saved the worlds."

"Huh. You're right, it does rock." She reached into a pocket on her brown leather jacket, producing a handful of badges on lanyards. "Here. These will let you and some friends come right up front when the show starts."

"Wow, thanks!"

I headed back to Izzy's booth, where we hung around through the readings. I knew it'd be a while before Night Creatures went on because they were all vampires, so once Logan's reading was done, I grabbed his hand and snuck off with him.

CHAPTER SIXTEEN

"I think we're alone now."

"What's going on, Aliyah?" Logan's voice was flatter than usual. He dropped my hand.

"Look, I wanted to apologize." I shook my head. "I mean, we got off to sort of an awkward start, and I felt like last night, you got embarrassed because of me."

"Awkward is kind of my default, though." He sighed. "I'm never gonna be chill like Hal or have game like Dylan. Or be good at faking it like Elanor. My parents hate it, but there's nothing I can do. And believe me, they've spent years plus tons of money trying to change practically everything about me. It's not you, it's me, and it always will be."

"Woah." I reached out to him again, taking him by the shoulder this time. "Hey. You're Logan, okay? You shouldn't try to be someone else, and I don't want you to be."

"Really?" He froze, his tension on hold but not gone yet.

"I mean it."

"But you don't like me? I mean, like-like, the way Grace likes Dylan."

"I never liked anyone before, not that way," I lied. Because now that the words were out of my mouth, I knew it wasn't true, but I couldn't come clean without hurting a lot of people's feelings. There was only one thing I could admit to, so I did. "It's nothing personal."

"It's not because I'm, you know." He closed his eyes and tapped his temple. "Slow."

"No, absolutely not." That was true. "I had no idea you were, actually, and it doesn't matter."

"Oh." He blinked. "Really?"

"I mean, you learn differently, but that's no big deal. And if your family gives you grief about that, remember, we're friends. We help each other, end of story."

"Peep!" Ember fluttered down from wherever she'd been flying and perched on my shoulder, snaking her neck out toward Logan. "Peep, peep."

"Okay." He looked Ember in the eyes. "I get it."

"Wait, you understand her?"

"Yeah." He nodded. "Most of the others, too."

"What did she say?"

"You don't know?" He blinked. "I thought every magus could understand their own familiar."

"Absolutely not. Logan, almost nobody has that talent." I grinned. "How long have you been able to understand critters like that?"

"Since my magic showed up a couple of years ago." He shook his head. "But my folks don't believe I can really do it."

So, Logan's parents hadn't just put him down and tried to squash him into the mold of their expectations, they'd totally dismissed his abilities. I swallowed the sudden flare of anger. Showing it would be futile right now, but if I ever got the chance, I'd give them a piece of my mind.

"I can't believe you don't know how rare your abilities are." I shook my head, picturing all my frustration rising up into the sky. I had to channel it somehow.

"Well, Ember asked me not to tell you what she said." Logan grinned sheepishly. "Which confused me, so thanks for the explanation, Aliyah."

"Hey, do you want to go and get some cotton candy or something?"

"Come to think of it, yeah, I do." His chuckle was higher-pitched than usual. "I didn't eat so much at lunch. Nervous, you know."

"Sorry about that. I should've talked to you last night." I sighed. "I was worried I'd hurt you because most of the time I care too much."

"It's okay, and I totally want us to be friends." He shook his head. "It's just, I felt weird because our whole group was pairing off, you know? I thought maybe we sort of had to get together because other-wise, we'd be the odd folks out."

"So, what are you saying here?" I blinked.

"I'm saying I like you. Aliyah, but not like-like." He nodded like he'd just made up his mind about it. "It's a good thing that you care too much, and I'm really glad we're friends. Honestly, it felt like I never had any until I came here. Not really."

"I'm glad we're friends, too. Come on, Salem's finest food trucks are waiting." I beckoned and he followed, Doris walking between us.

We held hands and it was totally platonic, almost exactly like walking around Salem with Izzy and Cadence practically my whole life. Logan should've had that growing up too, but it was okay to come late to friendship. True friends didn't care how long that took.

We spent about an hour sampling different foods and selecting the best treats to bring back to our friends. By the time we returned to Izzy's tent, Cadence had arrived. She had Brianna with her, plus a couple of guys who looked vaguely familiar.

Before I could ask for any introductions, Noah showed up. He was with Elanor, who stared at Logan and me. At first, I didn't know why until I remembered we were still holding hands. He let go before I did. I tried to hold on, but he wasn't having it. Maybe he was making the right call because once we stopped touching, she looked away.

"Aliyah." Noah's voice was low, almost reverent. "Night Creatures is playing, and we get to see them. Live! Can you believe it?"

"I know, this is awesome." I smiled because we were having a conversation that wasn't about our strained relationship or how choppy the social waters were at Hawthorn Academy. "But it gets better, Noah."

I rummaged in my bag, then dangled the lanyards. Noah's eyes went wide and his jaw dropped. If he weren't holding on to Elanor's arm, he might have fallen down.

"Are you serious?"

"Totally." I held out two of the passes.

"Thanks!" Noah couldn't move so Elanor took them, putting one around my brother's neck.

I made the rounds through my friends, handing out passes to each of them. Izzy declined; she had to man the booth. Cadence took one, but when I asked if I should go request a few more for her companions, she declined.

"I actually took this one for Brianna. Check it out." She pulled a press pass out of her jacket. "I'm covering this concert for the Gallows Hill school paper."

"Wow, awesome!" I directed my next question to the two guys. "Are you on the paper too?"

"Not exactly," the bigger of them said. He had a ring through his septum and a broad, stony face. "Let's just say we're in entertainment also."

"And you are?" Noah finally got his wits about him and raised his eyebrows at the two characters.

"Just a couple of lunks," the smaller one said with a shrug. His jet-black hair hung past his shoulders, softening the sharpness of his nose and jaw. There was something almost birdlike about him.

When I said larger and smaller, I meant that one was beanpole-thin, while the other was built like a Panzer tank. Both of them stood over six feet tall and were unsettling in a feral sort of way. I figured they were either shifters or changelings.

"All right." I shrugged. There was no point in asking more questions with this much evasion. Besides, they were with one of my best friends. How bad could they be?

"Aliyah? Don't you want to know who they are?" Noah blinked.

"Any friends of Cadence's are friends of mine."

"Thanks." Cadence grinned.

"Whatever." Noah shook his head. "The show's about to start, so finish your snacks on the way to the bandstand, okay?"

My brother's default was bossiness, but those were sensible enough instructions and we had no reason to protest them, so for once, my friends and I did what Noah said. It helped that Charity was nowhere to be seen. Surely, she had every reason to avoid a vampire concert.

Before the show went on, Michael Ambersmith got up in front of the mic stand. He didn't touch the band's equipment, though, because the Ambersmiths had all sorts of magipsychic devices, and right now, he used one to amplify his voice over the roar of the crowd.

"I'm here to call up our finalists in the costume contest."

Folks in the crowd milled about, making small talk. When he announced the five names, I wasn't surprised. Grace was. She jumped up and down, screeching in a way I'd never heard as she dashed toward the stage, up the steps, and all the way down the line of runners-up, which only made her costume seem more amazing. The rest of the contestants didn't have anything like that amount of mobility in their getups.

That was because Grace had used her magic while making it. I wasn't sure how she did it—maybe some technique learned in Quebec —but it paid off, judging by the awed gasps from the crowd.

This final round always got settled by a call for applause. Michael held his hand over each of the costumed heads, listening to and gauging the crowd's response.

When it was Grace's turn, practically the entire group from Hawthorn screamed at the tops of their lungs. So did everyone in Izzy's booth, and another huge section also cheered for her. At the front of this stood the two self-styled "lunks" with Cadence and Brianna.

Grace won. Michael handed her an envelope, which I knew contained several gift certificates from local shops and eateries, plus a bank check from the city for two hundred dollars. That was first prize every year for as long as I could remember.

She tucked that into her costume almost like an afterthought. I could tell that the real prize for her was acknowledgment. She had done something brilliant, and now everybody knew it. As she came back down to join us, her high color and springy steps told me Grace was totally elated.

Finally, it was time for the concert.

Up toward the front of the bandstand, there was a roped-off area that our passes let us access. It was as close as you could get to the wooden stage built on one side of the stone and metal structure. A bus with sunproof windows was parked across the common. That was where we first saw them.

Night Creatures was a punk band whose members were all vampires. They'd started back in the '90s when they were all still mortal and played regularly in Providence later that decade, but during the ten years after the Big Reveal, old vampires afraid of losing their powers went on a turning spree.

Lane Meyer and his friends got caught up in that disaster, ending up as second-class citizens like all the other vamps in this country. To this day, nobody was sure who'd arranged to have them turned or why. So, they changed the subject matter of their songs from dissatisfaction with a world that hid for so long to biting back against the flaws in this brave new society.

Noah had listened to them practically his whole life, which meant I had too. A handful of years ago, they'd gotten super popular after winning the Newport Battle of the Bands. Since then, they'd been in demand for appearances but didn't often play outside Rhode Island before graduating from Providence Paranormal. Now they had their degrees, and the Halloween gig in Salem was part of a short New England tour this winter. Next year, they'd go nationwide, so this might be the only time we'd see them in town.

There was an opening act, of course, but I didn't expect it to be one called Fred Redford and the Pixies. I'd had no idea he could even sing, let alone get up in front of a whole crowd of people like that. Everything I knew about him was from the news, mostly about how his intervention in the Under had helped foil my uncle's plans there.

Fred was actually pretty talented, although most of the crowd paid more attention to his dropped glamour. That's right, he went full Redcap for his performance. He was tithed to the Queen and Seelie but still totally scary. Redcaps were absolutely the sort of thing people wanted to see on Halloween in Salem. They had sharp sharkish teeth, gray skin, blazing red eyes, and of course, bloody red hats on their heads. Totally spooky and awesome in this town.

He sang a set of classic covers, the Halloween-type novelty music people played at parties. You know what I'm talking about—the *Monster Mash*, *Werewolves of London*, that sort of thing—but it was different from those old recordings. Sort of like a Postmodern Jukebox version, with a big band sound and bluesy vocals. At first, I didn't know where the instrumentals came from.

Turned out, he had a full complement of Pixies backing him up. Their tiny instruments were the real deal, and they used magic for amplification. Pixies were pure faerie creatures like Grims, but water-based and Seelie—perfect for Salem with its coastal charm.

Once Fred and company finished their set, he knelt, letting the Pixies climb up on his shoulders and arms so they could bow where everyone could see them. The gesture went along with everything I'd heard about the Tinfoil Hat folks—that they were determined and powerful, but also kind.

He got a good response from the audience, plenty of cheering and whistling, along with applause. I was glad for him; he deserved no less. But of course, everyone was really there for Night Creatures, and that was exactly what we got, plus a little something extra.

They had Irina Kaczynski join them on electric violin for three covers in their set. She was an internet-famous psychic fiddler. These were the songs they'd played the second night of their competition when she'd subbed in. This time, however, the guitarist and electric violinist performed together.

Everyone went nuts behind us—in a good way, of course. The covers went over well, exactly the sort of performance people loved here on Halloween. Usually, bands stuck to covers or their most popular songs. And for Night Creatures, that meant the ones that weren't blatantly about vampire rights.

Lane Meyer pushed the boundaries of the formula. This band was punk, which meant all their songs were political somehow. Even with their more understated tracks, they made a statement that was hard to argue with, but someone in the crowd had a different idea.

I didn't see the person in the horrifying costume earlier. They hadn't gotten passes like we had, but that didn't stop them. Earth magic quaked the ground, jostling everyone on it and knocking down the ropes. After that, the magus using it strode forward, mask covering their entire face. I noticed they had a familiar, something on the ground. I couldn't see it clearly in the dim light and commotion.

Riding the wave of the quake, a mound of earth lifted them above the rest of the crowd. This was some seriously powerful earth magic, stronger than I'd ever seen. Maybe it was because the autumn grass was thin in the Common, with more earth exposed. It let the magus manage something I'd never thought possible.

The quake rattled the bandstand.

Vampires had excellent reflexes, which was the only reason Lane and company were still standing. All the same, the drum set had toppled, and the bass drum had escaped its stand to roll around the stage. Irina fell backward, nearly cracking her head open on the marble. She would have been seriously injured if Fred hadn't gotten between her and the floor.

The magus on the mound didn't say a word. They didn't have to. Because they held an enormous sign. That and the costume made a blatant and ugly statement.

It was a vampire slayer's garb, as terrifying to folks with fangs as an SS uniform would be to anyone in my family. For five years after the Reveal, a group most people called terrorists but some considered vigilantes had gone around dressed in hoods and masks, stakes strapped to their chests. Any vampire they met got staked and decapitated.

That still happened on occasion.

That was one reason this magus was downright terrifying, but there was another. The sign they staked into the earthen mound was painted with fake blood, the kind you get in a costume store. It said this:

Burn All Leeches

In the other hand, they held a Molotov cocktail. And lit it.

They chucked it at the stage, aiming directly for Lane Meyer, the frontman of Night Creatures. He didn't duck, but faced the threat head-on, a matched set of birds taking flight from his fists. There was nothing else he could have done to fend off the fire arcing toward his flammable undead body.

"Hit it!"

It was Fred's voice, so the band didn't start playing, but he was one of the queen's knights, able to command her creatures. The Pixies jumped up from the railing they'd been sitting on during the Night Creatures set. All ten waved their hands in unison, and a matching gout of salty water flew toward the projectile.

The seawater slapped the bottle, crashing it into the wooden stage on top of the bandstand. It must have been filled with a mixture of oil and alcohol because it didn't go out right away.

Lane tried to stand his ground, hissing, fangs protruding as his vampiric instincts responded to the threat of an open flame. I recognized it. It was a magical fire, but not one cast by any magus. It was made from infused chemicals like we'd used that day in the lab.

Was the magus in the costume from my school?

The idea stole my breath. The next one was worse. What if it was a professor? Fear paralyzed me, but someone with more experience at working through that emotion snapped me out of it.

Logan grabbed my hand again. He directed his own jet of water at the blaze on the stage, and I knew his unspoken request. He wanted my help to banish the fire in case even more water couldn't extinguish it. I narrowed my eyes, glaring at the flames, and in moments, we'd put them out together.

"Security!" Fred Redford's voice roared from where he'd managed to sit up.

A group of burly figures clad in red ran out from the sides of the bandstand, dashing toward the costumed magus. As they turned, the back of their hood flipped up to reveal a ponytail. Before I could be sure of the hair's color, the attacker dove into the crowd.

"One, two, three!" Lane growled into the mic.

Matt the guitarist picked up his instrument and shredded out a sick riff. I recognized it; they were playing *Points*, their most defiant song. The drummer and the bassist joined forces, building a scaffold for the rest of the music. When Lane added his voice, the entire performance was a clear and present act of resistance in the face of terror.

> *"Without a doubt, I knew it sucked that night*
> *We'll never win, 'cause no one thinks we're right*
> *We had to walk away, and give up all our plans*
> *Why do I stop and turn around?*
> *And every time I smile they walk away from me*
> *A loser just because I'm fanged, you see*
> *And I'm seen as a guy with blood-lust rage*
> *Why am I stuck on this page?*
> *Eternity spent in a cage.*
> *What's the point again?"*

Salem's extrahuman community had a long memory because this town was steeped in a history of persecution. The immigration of the last surviving Morgensterns back in the 20th century only reinforced the attitude that we couldn't afford to tolerate intolerance.

So of course, the crowd sided with the vamps that night. Deafening applause marked the end of the song. My ears rang, and Ember hid her head in my hair. As it finally died down, my friends huddled together, hearts racing with fading adrenaline.

"We'd better get back to the school right away." Faith's voice was flat and hollow. "I'd bet dollars to donuts that was my megabitch sister. The headmaster will hear about this from me first."

She startled every one of us except Hal, who squeezed her hand and smiled at her. The crowd mostly dispersed, many disappearing as we stood there trying to catch our breath. Noah even stayed, although Elanor vanished into the crowd. It was almost an apologetic gesture.

I wasn't sure whether Faith was right. Charity was definitely a bullying bigot, but in the cafeteria, she'd waited until I turned on the magic. So far, she hadn't seemed like the sort who'd get her hands that dirty.

All the same, I hoped my brother would drop Charity like a hot potato the next day, but I didn't expect much. Courage didn't spring up fully formed overnight.

I'd hoped to meet more of my role models in person that night, but under the circumstances, I was relieved they left uninjured and safe, at least physically. They made their way to their bus under the park's municipal lighting. I watched them go, hoping that someday I'd have half their bravery.

The story continues with book three, *Fire of Justice*, coming soon to Amazon and Kindle Unlimited.

GLOSSARY

People

- **Changeling**- A mortal child of either one or two faerie parents. Most changelings choose a monarch sometime in their twenties, although some do it earlier than they have to.
- **Dampyr**- The mortal offspring of two vampires. They aren't as rare as many suspect, although because their blood is exceptionally sustaining to vampires, they keep their status secret. Dampyr sometimes have magic or psychic powers that work unreliably.
- **Faerie**- A term used to describe either a changeling who has tithed to a monarch and spent a year and a day in the Under or the pure creatures such as Gnomes and Pixies who were created by the king and queen.
- **Ghost**- A dead person with unfinished business becomes a ghost. If a mortal makes a contract before death, that gives them unfinished business and lets them linger. When ghosts finish their business, they move on, but no one knows where they go from here.
- **Magus**- A mortal who can use magic. Magic comes from

energy in the world. Most magi can only use one type of magic. However, a rare few can do more than one kind. Those are called extramagi.

- **Merfolk**- People who can live on land with legs or in the sea with fins and tails. They only emerged from the ocean after the Big Reveal and are still extremely rare outside of harbor towns.
- **Psychic**- A mortal with psychic power. Psychic ability comes from a person's own body and mind.
- **Vampire**- An unliving person who drinks blood to survive and enhance their abilities. Only regular mortals, psychics, and magi can get turned into vampires. Shifters, changelings, and faeries won't turn, and most of those won't survive an attempt.
- **Shifter**- A mortal who can take an animal's shape. Shifters have one form, with coloring similar to what they have while human. They usually have an enhanced sense while human-shaped, which goes along with their animal. For example, an owl shifter might have keen eyesight and a wolf shifter, a great sense of smell.

Shifter Varieties

- **Dragon**- The only shifters who can see both magic and psychic abilities, though only while shifted. The most powerful ones can partially shapeshift. Dragons are immortal and reproduce infrequently. There are so few of them since the Reveal that they've started taking other magical shifters as mates.
- **Kelpie**- A magical shifter who gets their abilities from an enchanted faerie pelt that bonds with their soul. The Kelpie pelts were created by the Goblin King, so they have Unseelie energy and restrictions. A Kelpie's animal form is a horse. Families pass the pelts down through generations,

and part of each ancestor lives on to help their descendants. The ancestors can get distracting, however.

- **Selkie**- A magical shifter who gets their abilities from an enchanted faerie pelt that bonds with their soul. The Selkie pelts were created by the Sidhe queen, so they have Seelie energy and restrictions. A Selkie's animal form is a seal or sometimes a sea otter. They can use water magic as long as they wear the pelt. Families pass the pelts down through the generations, and part of each ancestor lives on to help their descendants. The ancestors can get distracting, however.
- **Tanuki**- A magical shifter with enhanced speed and the ability to see all types of magic while shifted. They are also the only creatures who can manipulate luck, causing it to turn from good to bad or the other way around. They stop aging if they own a charm infused with luck from humans. Very few of those charms exist, having been either used up during the Reveal or locked away.

Powers

- **Air magic**- The power to conjure, control, and banish wind or air.
- **Earth magic**- The power to conjure, control, and banish earth, sand, or rock.
- **Empathy**- A psychic power to sense and influence emotions in other people.
- **Fire magic**- The power to conjure, control, and banish flames.
- **Ice magic**- The power to conjure, control, and banish ice.
- **Lightning magic**- The power to conjure, control, and banish lightning.
- **Poison magic**- The power to conjure, control, and banish poison. Each magus has a slightly different type of toxin they produce. Some are even antidotes to others.
- **Precognitive**- A psychic power to foretell future events.

- **Spectral magic**- the power to conjure, control, and banish light.
- **Spectral Affinity**- A trait some spectral magi have that makes them charismatic and believable.
- **Summoner**- A psychic power that lets the user make contracts with pure faeries, letting the summoner call them in times of need. Each creature has an anchor, some item symbolizing the bond. Mastery of summoning takes decades of study, which is why the most powerful are either vampires or past middle age.
- **Seelie**- The Sidhe queen's court. The Seelie way is about following the letter of the law, even when it's hard or cruel. They have a hard time reconciling faerie rules with the new mortal laws since the Big Reveal.
- **Solar Magic**- The power to conjure, control, or banish sunlight. Some of the most powerful practitioners can find hidden objects or discover long-kept secrets.
- **Solar Affinity**- A trait some solar magi have that makes them beacons for coincidence.
- **Space magic**- The power to move the self or objects instantly across distances. Some can even move other people.
- **Space Affinity**- This space power comes with an ability to locate people or things important to the magus.
- **Telekinesis**- A psychic power that moves objects.
- **Telepathy**- A psychic power to read minds.
- **Tithe**- The process of pledging to either the queen or king, making a changeling choose to be either Seelie or Unseelie.
- **Umbral magic**- The power to conjure, control, and banish shadows and veil or camouflage objects or people.
- **Umbral Affinity**- A trait some umbral magi have that makes them difficult to remember without psychic ability, faerie magic, or a shifter pack bond.
- **Undeath magic**- The power to conjure, control, and banish unliving energy.

- **Unseelie**- The Goblin king's court. The Unseelies bend the rules and often navigate mortal society more easily than their Seelie counterparts.
- **Water magic**- The power to conjure, banish, and control water.
- **Wood magic**- The power to conjure, banish, and control wood. It takes extreme power to influencing a living plant.

Creatures

- **Basilisk**- A venomous serpent that also has poison magic.
- **Dragonet**- A tiny dragon-like creature, always associated with one or more element which powers their breath attacks later in life. They have scales but are warm-blooded like birds. Most don't get much bigger than a small cat.
- **Familiar**- A magical or mythical creature who makes a bond with a magus.
- **Gryphon**- A chimera which has the head of a bird and hindquarters of a predatory mammal. They come in several combinations of base species, and habitat influences their choice in magi to bond with.
- **Karkus**- A crab that can change its shape. They're said to be the offspring of the crab that pinched Hercules as he battled the Hydra.
- **Lightning Bird**- A familiar from South Africa with an affinity for lightning. Its beak can jump-start a car.
- **Mercat**- A shapeshifting feline with fur for land and scales in the water. They can live in lakes, rivers, or in the sea as well as on land. They must never completely dry out, or they will die.
- **Moon Hare**- A magical rabbit that gets power from its particular moon phase. They commonly bond with umbral magi.
- **Pharaoh's Rat**- These natural predators of dragon shifters are the size of ferrets and resemble a mongoose with more

fur. They have an affinity for space magic and can use it on occasion.

- **Pigeon**- Not as mundane as most think, some pigeons have an uncanny sense of direction due to their affinity for air magic.
- **Pricus**- An aquatic goat said to be descended from Capricorn. They can warp time even better than Gnomes.
- **Pure Faeries**- Creatures who spring to life from magical sources in the Under. They are genderless, and their type and ability depend on place of origin. They're associated with only one court, although they will work together to defeat a common enemy.
- **Sand Cat**- A feline that lives in the desert, able to go for weeks without water. Earth magic lets them do this.
- **Sha**- A magical desert dog from Egypt. Sha are the size of mundane toy breeds with short hair and small pointy ears. They could pass for mundane except for their blue tongues. They are attracted to anything undead.
- **Sphinx**- A magic cat with an affinity for fire. The reason they're hairless is that they're resistant to flames.
- **Strix**- A venomous owl with an affinity for poison. Female striges have rounded tufts on their heads, while males have pointed ones.
- **Sumxu**- A lop-eared cat found only in northern China. They are masters of camouflage and have an affinity for several kinds of magic.

Places

- **The Academy**—Something between a community college and a military academy for extrahumans, the Academy is geared toward helping extrahumans who don't play well with mortals get ready to join a blended society. It's got divisions for learners of all ages, though they are housed separately.

- **Cherry Blossom School**- A dojo geared toward teaching extrahumans self-restraint, meditation, and how to temper their enhanced physical abilities with more mundane skills. It's been around for close to a hundred years, run by the Ichiro family. Mundane classes used to be offered as a front but now are a separate division.
- **Ellicot City Magitechnic**- A prep school for magi and psychics specializing in magipsychic technology. It's located outside Baltimore.
- **Gallows Hill School**- Traditionally for shifters, this prep school in Salem recently opened its doors to changelings and other extrahumans not categorized as magi or psychics.
- **Hawthorn Academy**- A preparatory school for magi in Salem. Its campus is in the space between the mortal realm and the Under, giving it unrivaled privacy. They specialize in teaching familiar magic.
- **Providence Paranormal College**- A school founded just one year after Brown University and located right in its shadow. Providence Paranormal used to admit only magi and psychics, but it's been accepting all types of extrahumans ever since Henrietta Thurston became headmistress. There has been trouble since then for students and faculty, leading people to believe dissenters are sabotaging the school.
- **Trout Academy**- A prestigious preparatory school for changelings with magic, recently open to magi and magical shifters. Its campus is located in South County and has been operating in some form or another since Rhode Island Colony was founded.
- **The Under**- The faerie realm. It's been divided into two parts ever since the Sidhe Queen and the Goblin king split up thousands of years ago. Mortals don't age in the Under, but it's a dangerous place for them to be. Getting lost means never being seen again, and it's easy to get indebted to

something nasty while trying to get through or out of the Under.

- **Wolf Messing Prep**- An institute for psychics to learn to control their skills before heading to college.

Events

- **The Big Reveal**- The term used for the 1990s, when the world discovered magic was real and extrahumans existed. The decade was marked with fear as everyone adjusted to the changes. Since the 21st Century, law and technology work for both humans and extrahumans.
- **Boston Internment**- A reaction by Boston government officials to the disappearance and suspected trafficking in extrahumans, especially shifters. All registered extrahumans in Boston lived on barges for close to a month under guard by the Boston Police. The traffickers got their hands on some magical gadgets, rendering the protection useless. Few survived.

THANK YOU!

Thank you for reading! If you loved this book, please leave a review. You can find my other work by clicking the links below, going to **my website** or visiting my **Author Central page**.

ALSO BY D.R. PERRY

Providence Paranormal College

Bearly Awake (Book 1)

Fangs for the Memories (Book 2)

Of Wolf and Peace (Book 3)

Dragon My Heart Around (Book 4)

Djinn and Bear It (Book 5)

Roundtable Redcap (Book 6)

Better Off Undead (Book 7)

Ghost of a Chance (Book 8)

Nine Lives (Book 9)

Fan or Fan Knot (Book 10)

Hawthorn Academy

Familiar Strangers (Book 1)

Acting in Kindness (Book 2)

Gallows Hill Academy

Year One: Sorrow and Joy (Book one)

For other books by DR Perry please see her Amazon author page.

CONNECT WITH THE AUTHOR

Website: https://www.drperryauthor.com/

Join her newsletter!

Find more of D.R. Perry's books on Amazon.

OTHER LMBPN PUBLISHING BOOKS

To be notified of new releases and special promotions from LMBPN publishing, please join our email list:

http://lmbpn.com/email/

For a complete list of books published by LMBPN please visit the following pages:

https://lmbpn.com/books-by-lmbpn-publishing/